Helena Patterson is a quiet and soft-spoken person who loves and appreciates her family as well as enjoys some quiet time alone, where she can focus on her creative side for story lines and ideas. She loves animals and enjoys spending time with her pets at home. She has an adventurous side and always seeks to explore new places and experiences with her wife, Tammy.

To Tammy: my soul mate, my inspiration, and my everything.

Helena Patterson

RANDOM ACTS OF VIOLENCE

AUSTIN MACAULEY PUBLISHERS™

LONDON • CAMBRIDGE • NEW YORK • SHARJAH

Ordering Information
Quantity sales: Special discounts are available on quantity purchases by corporations, associations, and others. For details, contact the publisher at the address below.

Publisher's Cataloging-in-Publication data
Patterson, Helena
Random Acts of Violence

ISBN 9781645751755 (Paperback)
ISBN 9781645751748 (Hardback)
ISBN 9781645751762 (ePub e-book)

Library of Congress Control Number: 2021902549

www.austinmacauley.com/us

First Published (2021)
Austin Macauley Publishers LLC
40 Wall Street, 33rd Floor, Suite 3302
New York, NY 10005
USA

mail-usa@austinmacauley.com
+1 (646) 5125767

Table of Contents

Chapter One
The Beginning

Julianne was working as a care-giver at the old age home in town. Although she had a nursing degree, she decided not to work as a nurse in a hospital again, because the hours were too long and left her no time for herself.

On a daily basis, she was required to administer the prescribed medication to the old people at the nursing home and when needed, assist the doctor with check-ups and giving flu-shots. This was something that she could handle easily and although she did not enjoy working with old people that much, she did try to make the best of it.

Julianne met Arthur at a club one night, while out with her friends. She was only twenty years old at that time. Arthur was a few years older than Julianne and was working at a steel factory and he was only there that night because his friends begged him to go with them, saying that he must get out more and with a lot of persuasion, he went with them. When Arthur saw Julianne on the dance floor, he almost instantly fell in love with her. He wanted to speak to her but he did not know what to say, so he walked over to her when the song ended and simply said to her, "I would really appreciate it if you allow me to buy you a drink." Arthur smiled at her and waited for a response.

Julianne looked at him and smiled. This was the first guy who treated her with some respect at a dance club and she could tell that he was not your regular Casanova, so she responded, "I don't allow strangers to buy me drinks, but if you tell me your name, you are no longer a stranger." She looked at him, waiting for his answer.

Arthur gave a huge sigh of relief. "Hi, I am Arthur, and you are?" he asked with a smile.

"I'm Julianne. Please to meet you, Arthur. I would take that drink now," she smiled back at him. That was how their friendship started. Julianne noticed that Arthur was a sweet guy and she knew that this was the kind of guy who would be loyal to her and although she usually preferred the more 'out-going' type of guys, she decided to give him a chance and so they started dating as a couple.

After a few months of dating, Julianne realized that she was pregnant. It was a shock to her because she still enjoyed her careless ways, going out whenever she had an opportunity and drinking and dancing with her friends every other night. Arthur did not like her going out so much, but he was not someone who enjoyed dancing so he allowed her to spent time with friends during the week whenever she wanted to.

When she broke the news to Arthur about her pregnancy, he was very excited. He always wanted to have a family of his own. He knew that this might just be what Julianne needed to settle down and act in a more mature way. He decided that they should get married before the baby was born, so they did.

Julianne did not have an easy pregnancy; there were a lot of complications with the baby and her health and every other week, Julianne had to go for check-ups at the hospital to ensure that she and her baby were doing well. This created a lot of tension and stress in their marriage and Julianne did not enjoy being pregnant at all. She could not wait for the baby to be born. This was when Julianne's depression started. Everyone told her that being pregnant should be the greatest thing for any woman to experience and this was just not the case in her situation. She was stressed out and depressed the whole time. Arthur refused her to go out and she was no longer allowed to drink and she also had to stop smoking. It felt as if she turned into a different person, whom she did not even recognize when she looked in the mirror.

It felt as if everything in her life had been turned upside down since her pregnancy.

After Ben was born, she felt a sense of relief and she promised herself not to have another child ever again. From then on, Julianne insisted that they always use protection.

Their marriage took a lot of strain when Ben was born and Julianne did not enjoy the responsibilities that came along with motherhood. She realized that she had no more time for herself and all her energy and time must be devoted to the baby. She had to quit her job and look after their son, which made her feel dependent on Arthur, which she did not enjoy one bit.

When Ben turned five, she told Arthur that she had to go back to work. She enrolled Ben in a day-care center and slowly but surely, all went back to normal again. Arthur could see the change in his wife's attitude and behavior and he was relieved to know that her depression subsided as soon as she started working again and Julianne was back to her old self within the next few months.

Years went by and Ben grew up to be a well-mannered child and he adored his mother and father. Everything seemed to be going well for the family until, one night, when Julianne became violently ill. She was rushed to the hospital and after the necessary blood tests was performed; the doctor informed her that she had an allergic reaction to craw fish and, "Oh yes, congratulations, you're six weeks pregnant," he said with a grin on his face.

Julianne was very upset after receiving the news. Arthur took his wife home that night and he was not allowed to talk about it on their way home from the hospital. Every time he tried to bring it up, she asked him to change the subject.

Julianne went to work the next day and the only thing that she could think of was how to get rid of this baby. She could not see herself going through all the pain and suffering again and could not imagine herself getting used to all the restrictions that she must face, again! She could imagine Arthur's voice telling her that she was not allowed to go out again or have a drink with friends.

When Julianne was pregnant with Ben, Arthur had all these rules that she had to obey. "No more drinking and partying, no more late nights out with your friends," Arthur used to tell her.

Now that Ben was older, she enjoyed the dinner and dancing with her friends again. Arthur would stay at home and look after Ben or they would get a baby-sitter when both of them went out for dinner. Everything was back to normal again and now this!

Julianne wanted to get an abortion but she knew that Arthur would never allow her to do that. If Arthur had not been in the room that night when the doctor informed her about her pregnancy, she would never have told Arthur and would have sorted out the problem by herself.

Julianne fell into a deep depression again and the only thing that she could think of was how to get rid of the baby. She wanted to induce a miscarriage. She started researching the subject online and she took all kinds of medication, such as strong pain killers, laxatives, everything she could get her hands on at work without anyone noticing. She did not tell any of her co-workers that she was pregnant. She was sure that she could make this go away before anyone noticed.

Chapter Two
The Arrival

Months went by and Julianne could see that her belly was starting to show underneath her clothes. She hated it. She would sit in front of the television at night and would press her fist hard into her stomach and she would hurt herself while doing this, but she did not care. She could not stand the sight of herself anymore, so she took a handful of pills and swallowed them down with a glass of vodka.

She no longer wanted to live and she could not stand going through everything again.

Ben went looking for his mom after he had a nightmare, and when he saw her passed out on the living room floor, he called the emergency number that he learned in school.

The ambulance came that night and took his mother to hospital and thanks to Ben, his mother and the baby were doing well. Julianne woke up in the emergency room in the hospital. She was not happy at all.

A few months after the incident, Julianne gave birth to a healthy baby boy. They named him Gregory.

Julianne and Arthur took Gregory home and Ben was waiting anxiously for his new baby brother to come home from the hospital.

When Ben saw his brother for the first time, he only wanted to hold him and play with him. This would be his new best friend, he thought to himself with a huge smile on his face.

Julianne hardly ever spent time with Gregory. She left him crying in his crib and she refused to breast-feed him. Arthur had to buy baby formulas at the pharmacy and he had to do everything for the new baby. Arthur took a few days off from work, so that the baby could be settled in at his new home. Ben was always around, helping his dad with his brother. He did not mind at all. He would check in on his baby brother whenever he got home from school and he grew very fond of Gregory.

Julianne refused to quit her job after Gregory was born and Arthur had to arrange for a nanny to look after the baby during the day. Arthur would make sure that Gregory was fed before the nanny arrived in the mornings, because he actually enjoyed having a baby in the house. He could see that Ben was just as excited and that made Arthur very happy.

Little did Arthur know that the new nanny was, in fact, highly addicted to heroin and most of the time, Gregory was left in his crib, unattended, and not taken care of until Ben came home from school. The nanny would leave as soon as Ben walked into the house, although she was told to stay until Julianne arrived home from work. Ben did not mind her leaving early, because he enjoyed spending time alone with his brother. Ben was now a nine-year-old boy, who had taken the responsibility onto himself to look after his baby brother. He would feed him, clean him up afterward, and change his diapers until his mom came home from work. He would then put Gregory back into his crib to go and do his homework and would come and check in on him every now and again. He could hear his brother crying when his mom was home but he soon realized that she did not spend time with his brother at all. She would put on her music in the kitchen while preparing dinner and would pretend not to hear the baby crying in the spare bedroom upstairs. Ben would go into the room and he would play with his brother until his dad returned home from work. Later on, Julianne terminated the nanny's contract and enrolled Gregory in a day-care center when he was two years old.

As the boys grew up, they became very close. It was clear to Ben that his mother did not give his brother much attention, even as he grew older. Whenever they got into trouble at home or at school, Julianne would punish Gregory far worse than she would ever have punished Ben for the same mistakes.

Quickly, Ben decided to take the blame every time that they got into trouble and knew that his punishment would be lesser than that of his brother. Gregory grew older and he soon realized that Ben was his mother's favorite. He knew that he could not do anything to change that, although he had tried many times. He started acting out to get her attention and that only made things worse between them. Finally, he gave up and that was when he had come to terms with the fact that Ben was acting as his protector whenever his mom would pick on him, which he started to appreciate more and more every day as he grew older. Although Ben meant well to cover up for all his brother's wrongdoings, it only showed Gregory that he never had to take responsibility for any of his actions or bad behavior. When

Gregory became a teenager, he had already developed some psychological issues and he had a lack of empathy and would constantly lie about anything and everything. It was almost as if he was playing a game with people. He wanted to see how far he could get without being caught out in a lie. He was able to predict how his family would respond to certain situations and he enjoyed taking advantage of it.

Chapter Three
Difficult Times

Ben was in his senior year in high school when his health started to cause him problems. He always enjoyed doing sports and did well academically, when, suddenly, everything changed. He told his mom that he recently felt tired and found it hard to concentrate in class.

Ben was taken to the doctor and the prognoses were dire. Ben was diagnosed with leukemia. Julianne was not coping at all with the latest news with regard to Ben's health and she quit her job to look after Ben in the final stages of his illness.

Gregory noticed that there was something seriously wrong with his brother's health and that caused him to act out in school; being more agitated and displaying erratic behavior toward the kids in his class. He was feeling depressed about the issue at home, but had no one to talk to about it and the only place where he could express this anger and anxiousness was at school. He would get into fights at school for no reason and he did not do his homework or listened to his teachers. Arthur was called to school a couple of times during the semester and he could not get Gregory to open up about his feelings.

Ben passed away at the early age of nineteen.

Julianne started drinking heavily and nothing would ever be the same in their family again. It felt as if she had lost her first and only child. Gregory's world came crashing down around him when his brother died. This was the first time that his parents noticed him crying. Ben was the only person in Gregory's world that was important to him. Ben was gone and Gregory felt alone.

Gregory was only ten years old but he knew that things would only get worse between him and his mother. He knew that she wished him dead, instead of his brother. He hated her even more for making him feel this pain and rejection.

Arthur thought that Julianne would go back to work a few months after the death of their son, however, Julianne did not seem to recover from this terrible incident. She walked around the house in her pajamas all day and refused to eat with them at the dinner table. She would go through to the kitchen, pour herself another drink, and would go straight back to bed. Arthur moved out of their bedroom, because he could not stand seeing her like this anymore. He begged his wife to seek help, go to a psychiatrist and therapy sessions, but she refused. Julianne was drinking every day and she carried a sense of sorrow around her that would even make the brightest ray of sunlight turn into something ominous and dark. Gregory knew that he had to stay out of his mother's sight when he returned home from school. He decided to hang around at his friends' house after school instead. He became friends with Mark last year and he noticed that he could easily manipulate Mark into doing anything he wanted him to do. Mark was a quiet kid with very low self-esteem and he had no friends. When Gregory noticed this, he easily worked his way into Mark's world. Mark was desperate for a friend, any friend, and Gregory knew this. Mark's parents recently got divorced and his mom had just started dating a new guy, named Joe. Mark's mom was working twelve-hour shifts since the divorce and she had to do this in order for her to keep food on the table. Mark missed spending time with his mom and when she started dating Joe, he felt even more alone than ever. Joe kept her away from him and his sister. Whenever his mom had a day off from work, Joe would make sure to take his mom out for the day, spending time alone with her, and he never invited Mark or his sister to join them, so it became clear to Mark that Joe did not like him and his sister very much. Mark's sister, Lucy, had just finished high school and decided to take a break for a while, before starting college next year. Lucy would take care of Mark when her mom worked until late in the evenings during the week and Gregory could relate to this, because Ben used to do the same for him, when they were growing up. Ben was always there for him whenever he needed to be taken care of. Gregory realized that he had more in common with Mark than what he had thought and he started to accept the fact and they became true friends, almost like brothers.

Gregory and Mark would go out into the woods behind Mark's house and Gregory would show Mark how to kill little insects and baby birds with rocks and sticks. Gregory realized that whenever he hurt something or killed something, it made him feel better. It was almost as if the act itself released the tension and anger which he kept inside.

Chapter Four
The Sacrifice

As Gregory grew older, his urge to hurt animals and people grew stronger and one day, he convinced Mark that if they killed Mark's dog, his mom would pity him and would spend more time with him, if he would follow through with it. Gregory knew very well that Mark desperately craved his mother's attention and that this might solve the problem for a little while. He could not listen to any more of his complaining about this issue; it was driving Gregory crazy.

The two boys took the dog into the woods and Gregory showed Mark how to slit the dog's throat using a stick and making an upwards motion around the dog's neck.

"Here, now you try it," Gregory said.

Mark knelt down next to his dog and took the stick out of Gregory's hand. He made the same movement as indicated by Gregory and looked back at his friend.

"Like this?" Mark asked in a hesitant tone of voice.

"Great!" Gregory responded. "Here, now, use the knife and do it for real."

He reached into his pocket and pulled out a knife and handed it to his friend.

Mark took the knife and looked at his dog. He started crying, "I can't do this. I love my dog. There must be another way for my mom to spend more time with us."

Mark got up and as he turned around to walk away from his dog, he heard a shuffle in the grass behind him and then a soft squeal. Mark turned around again and saw Gregory, on the ground with the knife in his hand, covered in blood. The dog lay lifeless on the ground next to Gregory. Gregory looked at Mark with a huge smile on his face. He felt a rush of excitement and relief going through his body as he slit the dog's throat. He was glad that Mark could not do it because he wanted to do it himself since they got here.

"There, I've done it for you!" Gregory looked proudly back at his friend. "Now, you can go home and tell your mom that the dog is gone and act real sad in front of her, I'm telling you it will work like a charm!" Gregory said, sounding very confident.

Mark looked down and realized that the dog really was dead and he started to cry. He did not want to hurt his dog; he did not think that Gregory would go through with it. Mark cried and walked back to his house, leaving Gregory behind in the woods. That night when Mark told his mom that he could not find his dog, they went into to woods to search for it together. The three of them looked around for a bit and when his mom came across the dog with his throat slit, Mark acted shocked and surprised. His mom was furious and could not understand who could have done such a cruel thing to a helpless animal. Mark went up to bed when they got home and he could not believe what he had seen today. It was horrific but Gregory was right about one thing, his mom did seem to be a bit more worried about him and his sister. A few weeks went by after the incident and his mom had been spending more time with Mark and his sister and less time with Joe and she even suggested that he can go to the kennels and get a new puppy.

"How did you know that my mom would spend more time with us if you killed my dog?" Mark asked Gregory a few days later at school.

"I just knew. People are so predictable," Gregory just smiled at Mark. He was glad that Mark was happy again.

Chapter Five

A Lesson Learned

Mark and Gregory were walking home from school one afternoon when some of the older boys in their school came walking up toward them. Gregory knew these kids; they were trouble-makers and always picked on the nerdy kids in school. They would threaten the younger kids to give them their lunch money or they would hurt them on the play grounds. Before Gregory and Mark became friends, he saw that they bullied Mark a few times as well, but then it did not bother Gregory as he did not know Mark.

"Oh no," Mark responded, as he realized who was walking up toward them. "These guys are trouble," Mark said in a panic-stricken voice to Gregory.

"I have seen them around you before, taking your stuff and smacking you around. Why do you allow that?" Gregory asked Mark. He could not understand why he never saw Mark fight back.

"What do you expect me to do? These are big kids and they always fight with everyone at school. I can't do anything to them. They will beat me up even more if I try to fight back," Mark said in an annoyed tone of voice. He did not want Gregory to judge him about this issue. He had never been a fighter.

"Mark, you must stand up for yourself or these kids won't stop targeting you. Don't you know that?" Gregory explained to Mark in a stern voice. He did not want these guys messing around with his friend anymore.

It seemed that this would be the day that Gregory would show Mark that the two of them could handle these bullies and that this would be another lesson that he needed to teach Mark. Gregory started increasing his pace as they walked toward the three guys in front of them.

"Gregory, what are you doing? Don't you see that they are coming straight toward us and we should turn around and run?"

Gregory could hear that Mark was in a panic and he was scared.

"Let's go into the alley and wait until they pass. We can come out again when the coast is clear," Mark pleaded with Gregory.

Mark thought to himself that he could not take another beating from these guys; he was still bruised up from the previous fight the other day, which he never told Gregory about.

"Sure," Gregory said with a grin on his face. They walked into the alley and Gregory knew that this would be the perfect spot to execute his plan. As the three kids came walking past the alley, Gregory yelled out to them in a mocking tone of voice, "Hi, fart faces!"

The kids stopped, looked at Gregory, and started walking toward him. "What did you say?" Dylan responded.

He was the one in-charge. The other two kids followed him around everywhere and did anything that he told them to do.

"Are you deaf and dumb?" Gregory responded with a huge smile on his face, waiting for Dylan to make the first move.

"What are you doing, Gregory!" Mark asked in a frightened voice behind him. He was hiding behind one of the garbage bins in the alley. "Why are you doing this? You know that they will beat us up because of what you've just said," Mark was angry at Gregory.

"Shut up, Mark! Stop being such a sissy, you need to show them that you can fight back!" Gregory responded in anger toward Mark.

"I can't fight, Gregory! Don't you get it?" Mark yelled back at him.

"No, Mark. You just never tried," Gregory said and walked over to the dustbin to grab a piece of rustic pipe and started swinging it in front of him, mocking Dylan to come closer.

Dylan laughed as he walked toward Gregory. He was a seventeen-year-old teenager with an athletic built and was part of the wrestling team in school. He looked at Gregory and thought to himself that he just about had it with these ugly, pimple-faced juniors in his school, who walked around like a bunch of nerds, not knowing what to do with themselves because they were so boring! This kid needed to be put back in his place and he would make sure that from now on, he showed some respect to the seniors in school after he was done with him today!

He walked up to Gregory and grabbed the pipe out of his hand. He hit Gregory across the face with the pipe and Gregory fell to the floor. Dylan threw down the pipe and started beating Gregory in the face while he was lying on the floor. Dylan's friends just stood and watched as the scene unfolded.

"Get up, you prick!" Dylan yelled out to Gregory, who was still lying on the floor. Gregory could feel something warm running down his nose and as he wiped it off with his hand. He realized that his nose was bleeding. Gregory smiled and got up. He walked toward Dylan and as Dylan reached to grab Gregory, Gregory threw a punch straight into Dylan's stomach. Dylan crunched forward and Gregory grabbed Dylan's head and brought it down toward his knee in a quick and effortless motion; Dylan fell to the floor. The other two kids who were with Dylan just looked on as the fight continued. They did not want to get into a fight today, after all, Dylan should be able to get back on his feet soon and beat the crap out of the little guy. Dylan got up and grabbed Gregory around the waist and brought him down to the ground in a hard thud. The kids started laughing; thinking that this was what they were waiting for. Dylan was now on top of Gregory and punching him in the stomach and ribs. Gregory could see the other two kids walking off, out of the alley.

One of them yelled to Dylan, "We will hear about it at practice, Dylan! Finish him off and meet up with us soon!" They laughed and disappeared around the corner. Mark was sitting in a corner near the dust-bin, crying. Gregory saw this and he got so furious because if Dylan had a chance to tell his story at school tomorrow, they would both be laughed at. Gregory wanted Mark to join in the fight and give him a chance to defend himself, but Gregory could see that this was never going to happen. Mark was right; he was just not a fighter.

Gregory stretched out his arm toward the pipe, which was inches away from him, and as soon as he could reach it, he grabbed it and hit Dylan across the shoulders with it. Dylan tried to wrestle it out of Gregory's hands but Gregory held on to it as tight as he could and he was using his legs and all of his strength left in his body to roll over on top of Dylan. Now the roles had been reversed and Gregory managed to have Dylan pinned down on the ground with the pipe pushing down onto Dylan's neck.

Gregory was pushing harder and harder on Dylan's neck and he could see that the area around Dylan's mouth appeared to be changing to a light blue shade, his eyes were full of fear, and Gregory could see that his eyes got wider and wider. The more he struggled to get lose from Gregory's grip, the more powerful it made Gregory feel. He loved this feeling of being in total control and within a matter of minutes, Gregory could feel Dylan's body going limp underneath him. Dylan was lying on the ground, eyes still wide open, but no longer breathing.

"Yes!" Gregory yelled out excitedly. He looked up to see if Mark was still in his corner and yes, there he was, his head on his knees, covering his ears with his hands. He was shaking and crying.

"Mark, get up. It's over." Gregory said out loud as he walked over to Mark. Mark looked up and saw Gregory walking toward him. His face was covered in blood but he was smiling from ear to ear. Dylan was still lying on the floor, motionless.

Gregory must have knocked him out or something, Mark thought to himself.

"So, you won?" Mark asked in disbelief.

"Yup! Let's just say that he won't be bothering us anymore," Gregory smiled and they grabbed their school-bags and walked out of the alley. Mark did not get a good look at Dylan but he was sure that when Dylan would wake up, he would be totally pissed at Gregory.

Dylan never woke up again.

Gregory went home that day feeling very proud of the fact that he was able to help Mark with another issue he had. Gregory knew that he had to look out for Mark the same way that his brother, Ben, always looked out for him.

The next day, the kids in school noticed that Dylan did not turn up for class. Everyone assumed that his family must have moved away and no one really missed having him around. They were glad that the bully was no longer attending their school. Mark could not understand what was going on when he heard the news about Dylan but Gregory reassured him that he probably told his parents that he no longer wished to be in their school, because what would the kids think if they knew that a junior had beaten him up the day before. Mark laughed and agreed with Gregory; that did make a lot of sense to him. A few days later, news reports revealed that Dylan's body was found in an alley by a homeless guy. The police were still investigating the issue but they believed that it must have been a drug related issue.

Chapter Six
White Lies

As the months went by, Gregory and Mark's friendship grew stronger. Gregory was almost always at Mark's house and Gregory's dad was starting to worry about his son. He is never home anymore and his wife no longer knew what day of the week it was, she was mostly up in their bedroom; sleeping or drinking.

Arthur decided to speak to his wife again about seeing a psychiatrist. After days of pleading and begging, she finally agreed and when Arthur and Julianne went to see the psychiatrist, he recommended that Julianne should be admitted to a rehab facility for at least one month in order for them to ensure that she receives the right care and medication during the treatment process. Julianne agreed, not because she wanted to get better, no, she agreed because she just could not stand to be in her house anymore. Everywhere she turned; she could still see Ben and sometimes even hear his voice. That was why she could not leave her bedroom; the memories of her beloved son were everywhere around her and that was driving her crazy. She would be glad to have an excuse to get away from Arthur and Gregory as well, because they did not seem to understand what she was going through. They just went on with their lives and it seemed to her that they had already forgotten Ben and that made her mad. She couldn't stand being around the two of them.

Arthur felt relieved to know that Julianne agreed to be admitted and he was glad to know that his wife was in a place where they would be able to help her through her struggles.

When Gregory came home from school that day, Arthur informed him that his mother would be gone for at least a couple of weeks. Gregory felt elated. Finally! He could move around in his house without feeling tense and nervous the whole time. He knew his mother hated him and he wished that she would never return home again.

Mark was invited for a barbeque at Gregory's house for the first time. Arthur wanted to meet his son's friend and he arranged for the kid to come over for a visit.

The day went well without any incident and Arthur noticed that Mark was a well-mannered kid and he seemed to be a good influence on Gregory. That night, the boys were playing pool in the games room when Mark's sister phoned him. She was crying and she was asking if Mark could arrange for Gregory's dad to come and pick her up at her boyfriend's place. They got into a fight and she didn't want her mom to know about it. Gregory asked his dad if he could help and Arthur immediately grabbed his car keys and the three of them went to fetch Lucy, Mark's sister. She was waiting on the corner of the street for them to come and pick her up. When she saw Gregory's dad's car, she quickly ran toward it and was waving them down to pull-over. She did not want any more trouble tonight, so she decided to sneak out of Dennis's house when he went to the kitchen to fetch another beer. "Thanks, Mr. Smith. I did not know who else to call," Lucy said gratefully as she climbed into the back seat of the car.

"Not a problem, Lucy. I'm just glad that you phoned your brother."

Arthur turned around to look at the girl, who was speaking to him, and saw the bruises near her eye and on her cheek. Arthur immediately felt concerned for her and pulled over.

"Did he hit you?" he asked her.

"Don't worry, Mr. Smith. I have told him that this will be the last time that he raises his hands toward me," Lucy responded, tears rolling down her cheeks. She felt ashamed of what had happened.

"You mean this is not the first time?" Arthur asked her again; he was very concerned for her safety.

He wished that he could get hold of this guy and teach him a lesson or two. Mark looked at his sister's face and then gave her a big hug, "Don't worry, sis. We will make sure that he never hurts you again, isn't that right, Gregory?"

He turned his gaze to Gregory.

"That's for sure! He needs to be punished for this, right, Dad?" Gregory asked his dad, sounding almost excited about the idea.

"He will be punished, boys. Don't worry. Lucy, we will take you the police station to report this incident and then they will handle this matter in the right way."

Arthur re-assured the boys.

Lucy didn't want to get Dennis into trouble, she still loved him, but she knew that she had to play along at the moment or else this man might tell her mother about the incident. She didn't want that to happen.

Arthur stopped at the police station and just as he was about to get out of his car to escort the girl, Lucy said that she and her brother will go in together to report this. Arthur and Gregory stayed in the car, as they watched Lucy and her brother walk into the police station.

"Dad, what will the cops do to Dennis?" Gregory wanted to know what punishment would be given to Dennis after he had seen poor Lucy's face.

"They will charge him with assault and he could even go to jail. The good thing about this is that the police will be made aware of Dennis and his bad behavior," Arthur replied confidently.

Gregory looked at his dad and said, "I don't know if that is enough punishment for him. He did hurt Lucy and that does not sound like real punishment to me." Gregory was not happy with what the police would do. It seemed to Gregory that Dennis would just get a slap on the wrist for what he had done to Lucy.

"That's how the law works, son. Don't worry, they will sort him out," Arthur tried to reassure his son.

Meanwhile, Lucy and Mark walked into the police station and to Lucy's relief, the police officer at the front desk was having a very busy night. He did not even notice them walking through the front doors. People were standing and talking everywhere and it was loud and chaotic.

Lucy grabbed her brother's hand and dragged him toward a quiet corner in the police station. "Mark, let's just go home. You can see that these officers are busy with far more urgent matters than my foolish fight with Dennis," Lucy explained to her brother, hoping that she could convince him to avoid laying charges against Dennis. "Let's just walk out and tell Gregory's dad that I have filed a report and that everything has been sorted out. Please, Mark, I'm so tired, I just need to go home," Lucy pleaded with her brother.

Mark looked at his sister and he could see that there were tears in her eyes. The bruises on her face looked painful and he could imagine that she just wanted to be at home, in bed. He knew this feeling too well.

Besides, he did not want to force her to do anything that she did not want to do.

"I understand how you feel, believe me," Mark replied, thinking about Dylan, who had bullied him at school before, and he hugged his sister and they walked out of the police station.

"Everything sorted out?" Arthur asked as they climbed back into the car.

"Yes, thank you, Mr. Smith. Can we go home now? I'm so tired," Lucy replied quickly.

Arthur dropped the two kids off at their house and he and Gregory drove home; it felt good to know that he was able to help one of Gregory's friends today.

Chapter Seven
The Final Straw

Days went by and Gregory could see that Mark was distant and pre-occupied with thoughts. "What's going on, Mark?" he asked Gregory as they walked home from school that day.

"It's nothing. Just forget about it," Mark quickly responded. They walked off in silence.

The next afternoon, Gregory's dad asked him to buy bread and milk at the corner shop after he had done his homework. He walked to the corner shop and decided to stop by at Mark's house to see if his friend was feeling a bit better. Gregory knew that something was wrong with Mark but he did not want to push the subject any further the other day, so he left it at that. Gregory knocked on the door and Lucy answered. She had a lot of make-up on her face, more than usual, and Gregory could see the black and purple discoloring on her skin underneath the make-up around her left eye. It also seemed to be swollen.

"Hi, Lucy, is Mark here?" Gregory asked, not wanting her to feel uncomfortable around him; he pretended not to have noticed the bruises on her face.

"Hi, Greg, yes, he is watching television. You can go through to the living room," she said with a smile and showed him in.

Gregory walked in and saw his friend sitting on the couch, watching television. Mark looked up and when he saw Gregory, he looked shocked.

"What's up?" Gregory said, as he walked over to Mark.

"Hi, Gregory, didn't expect you to come over today," Mark quickly replied, looking down at his hands. He knew that Gregory must have seen his sister's face and he did not know what to tell his friend about that. He still felt guilty for lying to Gregory and his father the other night.

"I had to stop by the store, so I popped in to see if you wanted to play video games," Gregory said with a smile.

"Sure, why not," Mark got up and they went to Mark's room.

When they entered the room, Gregory asked Mark about his sister's black eye.

"I thought that the police had sorted him out?" Gregory was confused.

"Gregory, please don't be angry but she did not go through with it the other night. She just wanted to go home and the place was packed with people, so I am sure she felt ashamed."

Mark wanted to stand up for his sister. It's hard for anyone to understand this type of situation, unless you've been through it yourself.

Gregory looked at Mark in disbelief. He was sure that this was the first time that his friend had ever told a lie to him. He was disappointed. Just as he wanted to say something to Mark, the bedroom door opened and Lucy came walking in. "Gregory, please don't be upset with my brother. I know that he must have told you already?" Lucy looked at Gregory. It was clear to him that she felt bad about lying to his dad.

"I told him that we should leave the police station that night, I did not want Dennis to get into trouble because he could lose his job if I went through with it. I am so sorry that I lied to you and your dad," Lucy had tears in her eyes again.

"But look at your face!" Gregory could not understand why she allowed Dennis to hurt her again. "Why do you allow him to beat you up like this?" Gregory asked, feeling angry about the whole situation again.

"It's none of your business, Gregory! You are just a child! You can't possibly understand my situation!" Lucy was angry and she felt ashamed because she could not even answer that question to herself.

"Oh, please, that is nonsense and you know it!" Gregory yelled out in anger.

Just then, Dennis came walking in with a beer in his hand. "Lucy, stop hanging around these two losers and go make me a sandwich," he glared over at Mark and Gregory and walked out of the room into the hallway.

"You're seriously not going to make him a sandwich, are you?" Gregory was furious.

"Gregory, stop being so childish, I don't have to explain myself to you!" Lucy replied; she was getting annoyed with this kid. She turned around and walked out of the room toward the kitchen. Gregory looked at Mark in disbelief.

"I know, I know. This is what I was trying to tell you earlier. There is just no way to get through to my sister. She keeps saying that she loves him and honestly, I don't know why or how she can love something like that!" Mark replied in disgust.

"I see that now," Gregory said, feeling so annoyed and confused at the same time. Lucy walked into the kitchen and Dennis was sitting at the kitchen table, waiting anxiously for her to make him a sandwich. "Come on, woman, I don't have all day! You are so slow; you must have been dropped on your head a few times when you were a baby!" Dennis said in a sarcastic tone of voice and started laughing at Lucy.

"That was not necessary to say those things, Dennis. You are so mean to me sometimes!" Lucy said angrily back at him.

Dennis stood up and walked over to her, grabbed her hair on the back of her head, and pulled it hard toward the floor. He whispered in her ear in a threatening tone of voice, "Listen, I can talk to you however I choose to. You do not ever talk back to me again, do you understand?" Dennis was clenching on his teeth as he spoke to Lucy and while he was speaking, he was pulling as hard as he could on her hair and he enjoyed the fact that she was scared of him.

Just as Dennis was saying this to Lucy, Gregory walked into the kitchen to fetch a soda for himself and Mark. He stood quietly in the kitchen door and watched the situation unfold in front of him. He knew then that the reason why Lucy did not report Dennis to the police was not because she was worried about him losing his job. It was because she was worried about what he would do to her if she went through with it. Gregory could see that Lucy was afraid of Dennis. She was pale in her face and he could see that she was shivering while he stood there, saying those things in her ear, twisting her hair around his knuckles in his hand.

Gregory could feel his rage getting the better of him and his hands felt cold and he realized that he was clenching his fists tightly.

Dennis saw that Lucy was looking at something behind him and when he turned around, he saw Gregory standing behind him.

"What are you looking at? What do you want?" Dennis yelled at Gregory, making a fist, and pointing it toward Gregory.

Gregory looked at Dennis, walked straight past him, took a glass from the kitchen counter, and poured himself a glass of water. He turned around, looked at Lucy and said in a calm voice, "I don't know what you see in this guy. He has the face of a donkey and he smells like shit." Gregory looked back at Dennis and he could see Dennis's face turning red with anger.

Gregory gulped down his water and in a split second, Dennis was standing in front of him and his face was inches away from Gregory's face. Gregory knew what was coming next, so in one swift move, he smashed the glass in his hand on the kitchen basin next to him and as Dennis turned to look at what just happened, Gregory thrashed the broken piece of glass into Dennis's left eye socket.

Dennis screamed out in pain and grabbed his face in his hands; he did not even realize what just had happened. Blood was running down his face and Lucy just looked at Gregory in shock. She did not move; she did not say a word.

"How does that feel, Dennis?" Gregory asked softly, standing behind him, whispering in his ear, just as he had done with Lucy a few minutes ago.

"See, you can't just go around hurting people and think that it's okay. Did you not think that, one day, someone might just return the favor?" Gregory asked Dennis with a grin on his face. Gregory turned around and looked at Lucy, she was still standing there, and she seemed to be frozen in time.

"You can take him to hospital or you can ask him to leave you the hell alone. This is now your choice," Gregory said to Lucy as he walked past her toward the kitchen door. He was smiling from ear to ear this time.

Mark came walking in just as Gregory walked past Lucy with a big smile.

Lucy looked at Dennis and then said in a calm tone of voice, "You better go, Dennis. Don't ever come back again."

"Lucy! You need to help me, please, my eye!" Dennis pleaded with Lucy.

"Just leave my sister alone, Dennis!" This time it was Mark who was talking loud and clear. He did not want this man ever coming near his sister again.

"Screw all of you!" Dennis yelled out as he stumbled out of the kitchen.

I will be back, that's for sure! They have not seen the last of me yet! Dennis thought to himself as he stumbled out the front door toward his car.

Mark looked at Lucy and Lucy looked back at her brother and his friend. They all started laughing. They were not sure if it was from shock or from relief from knowing that Dennis had just gotten what he deserved, finally!

Lucy walked over to Gregory, put her arms around him, and said, "What is wrong with you? You are one crazy teenager." She smiled and gave him a big hug, "You know he could have hurt you, don't you?"

Gregory looked up at Lucy and smiled, "I don't care. I had to teach him a lesson."

"My Hero!" She smiled at Gregory and she felt so relieved that it was all over.

Chapter Eight

The Return

The month came to an end and Gregory knew that his mom would be returning home soon. He felt gloomy about this fact and he wished that he had some place else to stay instead.

Julianne was unpacking her clothes and she had to admit that the treatment center helped her a lot. She almost felt like her old self again. She looked out of her bedroom window and saw Gregory walking up the driveway toward the front door. He was home from school, but he did not know she was already home today.

She opened the front door just as he reached out to open it and he saw his mother standing in front of him.

"Hi, Gregory," Julianne said politely to her son.

"Hi," he quickly responded and brushed past her to go to his room. Julianne did not expect a 'warm welcome' from her teenage son but she was not impressed with the way he had just treated her. She wanted to make things right with Gregory and she knew that it would take some time and effort to do that. Gregory was busy in his room when he heard a knock on his bedroom door. "Come in," he said, looking at his mother as she entered his room.

"Gregory, I wanted to ask if I can fix you something to eat," Julianne looked at her son.

He looked up at her, standing there, looking uncomfortable and insecure.

"No, I'm fine, thanks. I'm going to Mark's house after I've done my homework," Gregory quickly replied.

"Oh, is he one of your friends?" Julianne asked again.

"He is my only friend, not that you've noticed these past two years," Gregory replied sarcastically.

He was irritated and he could feel his hands getting cold and sweaty. He was angry and he wanted her to leave him alone.

"You're right, Gregory! I did not pay much attention to you and your friends because I was too busy looking after your sick brother! Not that you noticed that at all!" Julianne had lost her cool and she was angry and upset and she could not keep the words from rambling out of her mouth.

"You have no idea what I have gone through these past couple of years. I am trying to be a better person and mother, but you make it so hard for me!" Julianne replied again. She just could not seem to get through to Gregory.

She looked at Gregory and he was sitting on his bed, looking at her with a blank expression on his face. He felt cold toward her and she could see that he seemed a lot older than what she remembered him to be and he looked almost too mature for his age.

"I am sorry. I did not mean to yell at you," Julianne felt guilty and apologized to Gregory. She did not mean to snap at him like that. Gregory looked back at his mom and could not believe what she just said. She had never apologized to him before.

She must be on some sort of medication, he thought to himself. "I'll be home later," Gregory said as he stood up and walked past her out into the hallway.

He couldn't stay here; he had to go somewhere else. He had to calm down.

Julianne watched as her son walked out the door again. She knew that this would not be easy but she thought that Arthur would at least be happy to see her. She went to the bathroom to wash her face and decided that she would make some dinner for them and then try again later that night to have a decent conversation with her son.

After all, he was just a kid and he would never understand what she had gone through. Losing a child is the worst kind of pain any parent could ever experience. She went into the kitchen and started preparing dinner.

Arthur came home and was clearly happy to see his wife again. She seemed to be doing better and she even prepared dinner for them, which she had not done in years.

The three of them were sitting around the dinner table, quietly eating their food. "So, sweetheart, how are you feeling?" Arthur asked politely.

"I am feeling much better. I've learnt so much these past few weeks," Julianne replied with a smile.

Gregory was watching both of his parents, quietly eating his dinner, which was not bad, at all. He did not even know his mom could prepare a plate of food like this. He could not help feeling anxious; he had seen it too many times before. One moment, everything seemed peaceful and calm and then, after his mom had a few drinks, all hell would break loose.

She was drinking water tonight, but he knew, it wouldn't be long before she would be back to her old habits again.

"Did you decide on what you're going to do, honey?" Arthur asked. He wanted to know if Julianne had given it much thought to go back to work, which he thought would be good for her.

"What do you mean?" Julianne asked, sounding annoyed with her husband.

"Are you going back to work next week? The reason why I am asking is because Celia phoned me yesterday; they cannot seem to manage without you," he said with a smile. His wife really did a good job while working at the care facility a few years back and good help was hard to find these days.

"They have another opening, if you are interested?" Arthur replied again.

"You're kidding me, right? I just got home today and already you want to send me back to work!" Julianne responded angrily.

"Of course not, honey. I'm sorry. I did not mean to upset you," Arthur apologized.

"I thought that you might get bored at home and I only mentioned it to you just in case you might be interested," Arthur explained.

"Yes, why on earth would I want to be home all day? Do you realize that I had never had any time for myself? I had to look after Ben because you did not want to take precious time off from your job to look after your own son! And after Ben passed away, I had no one left!" Julianne responded in a fit of rage. "These past few weeks were the only time that I could relax and take care of myself for once!" Julianne could feel the urge to drink was getting stronger and she had lost her cool completely.

Gregory pushed his plate out in front of him, stood up, and walked out of the dining room. "Same old, same old," he said as he walked out.

"Julianne, please, calm down," Arthur pleaded with his wife.

He didn't know how this conversation got out of hand so quickly.

Julianne sat quietly, looking out in front of her. Her doctor told her that the first day back would be the hardest. "I need to phone my sponsor," Julianne stood up and walked over to the phone in the kitchen.

Arthur started clearing the table. This is the least I can do, he thought to himself.

He started doing the dishes and he could hear his wife crying and complaining about her situation at home. He looked out the kitchen window and thought to himself that things were so much better when Julianne was not around. Would she ever get better? He could not imagine that she would ever change.

Julianne walked back into the kitchen, put on the kettle, and walked over to Arthur. "I'm sorry. I just need to take things slow for a while," she explained to her husband. She put her arms around her husband and they stood there holding each other for a few seconds in silence.

"I understand. I should not have brought up the subject about work. I did not mean to upset you," Arthur apologized again.

Julianne looked at her husband. "I am sorry, too. I should not have snapped at you like that. I have arranged with Shaun to see him tomorrow. He suggested that I continue with a daily session at his office, at least for the next two weeks. This is just to make sure that I stay on track with my recovery," Julianne informed Arthur.

"Sounds good, honey, I am so glad that you have phoned him," Arthur felt relieved; maybe, this might work out fine after all.

Julianne went to see Shaun Reilly who had been assigned to her case when she was admitted to the rehab facility. The more time she spent with Shaun, the more comfortable she started feeling around him. She truly shared all her fears and dreams with him during their therapy sessions and it felt as if Shaun understood her better than Arthur ever did.

During one of their sessions, Julianne confided in Shaun about her disappointment in Gregory. "I have apologized to him the first day I came back and do you know what he did?" Julianne started. "He just ignored me! He did not even say that he had missed me while I was away for that month. I could never seem to please that child." Julianne felt sorry for herself and started crying. She was sure that Gregory would try to be a better son to her when she got back but he only seemed to be more distant toward her than ever before.

"Ben was always nice to me and he always tried to please me," Julianne continued. Julianne never realized that Ben was actually a very anxious child around his mother, after Gregory was born.

He only wanted to keep his mom happy and wanted to keep his brother out of harm's way. When it came to the relationship between his mom and his brother, Ben noticed that Julianne did not want to spend time with Gregory at all; she just did not care for him. Julianne didn't want to see that she, in fact, was the wrongdoer in the family. Shaun suggested that Julianne must try to spend more time with Gregory. She should schedule a movie night for them or try to get to know his friend a bit better. So, that afternoon, when Julianne got home after her therapy session, she started baking some cupcakes and mince rolls for the movie night which she had planned for them.

Chapter Nine
Good Intentions

Gregory came home from school and saw his mom busy in the kitchen, preparing food.

"Hi, Mom," he said as he entered the kitchen.

"Hi, Gregory, I have decided that we will have a movie night tonight. See, I am busy baking some cupcakes for us to enjoy while we watch the movie. It's going to be fun; don't you think?" Julianne said, smiling at Gregory.

Gregory looked at his mother, not sure what to think of this whole idea. She had never done anything like this before.

"Oh, alright," he quickly replied and turned around to walk out of the kitchen.

"Oh, alright? Oh, alright? Is that all you have to say?" Julianne snapped at Gregory.

"What do you want me to say, Mom?" Gregory snapped back at her. "You know that I'm not seven anymore, right?" he continues=d. "I don't think you realize how old I am sometimes! I don't even like cupcakes that much, but if you insist!" Gregory yelled back at his mom.

He had had enough of her mood swings and temper tantrums. He had held onto this anger for too long, he was so tired of her nonsense. How dare she pretend that everything was great when she knew that it wasn't and it would never be!

"Go to hell, Gregory! You are a selfish, spoiled little brat!" Julianne yelled back. As he turned to leave the kitchen, she grabbed the baking tray in front of her and threw it across the room toward Gregory. Cupcake dough went flying out of the baking tray and onto the kitchen counter and floor. "And you can clean up this mess! I'm sick and tired of cleaning up after you and your dad. Both of you make me miserable!" Julianne yelled out and grabbed her car keys and hand-bag. Gregory stood there in silence. This is the mother that I've known all my life. No therapy will ever change her, he thought to himself.

Julianne left the house, not knowing where she was going, but she knew she can't stay one minute longer in that house. She decided to meet up with Shaun for coffee. She desperately wanted to see him and talk to him; he was the only person who seemed to understand her.

She waited for him at the diner while drinking her coffee. The waitress walked past her with two beers on a tray and Julianne had a sudden urge for a drink.

"May I have one of those?" Julianne asked her as she walked past, pointing at the beer on the tray.

"Sure, I'll be right back," the waitress replied politely.

Julianne knew that she should not have a drink but she also knew that no one was around to tell her 'no.' Shaun phoned and told her that he would not be able to meet up with her because his wife had just informed him that their daughter got hurt at school and he needed to go to the hospital urgently. He would send her another sponsor to talk to in a few minutes.

"No, don't be silly. I am feeling much better already," Julianne quickly replied while looking down at the glass of beer in front of her. "I understand. Family should always come first, right?" she responded with a false smile on her face. She never even knew that Shaun was married. He did not wear a wedding band and she couldn't remember seeing any family photos in his office.

"Are you sure, Julianne?" Shaun asked, sounding concerned for her.

"Yes, I'm fine. I'm having a cup of coffee as we speak," Julianne lied, but she did not care anymore. Just then, the waitress walked past Julianne again and she pointed to her, indicating that she must bring another beer to the table as her glass was almost empty already.

"Bye, Shaun, I will speak to you again in the morning," Julianne quickly responded and dropped the phone. She took the last sip of beer and she could feel the anger and anxiousness disappear for a split second. She smiled and drank another one.

Arthur came home from work and was happy to know that his wife called him earlier and planned a movie night for the three of them.

The house seems too quiet, he thought as he entered the hallway. He went into the kitchen, saw the mess on the floor and kitchen counter, and did not know what to think at first. He looked around and found the baking tray underneath the kitchen counter in the corner. He walked over to pick it up and put it back on the counter. Julianne must have had an episode again, he thought, giving a loud sigh and shaking his head from side to side. Not again.

"Julianne! Gregory!" he called out as he walked through the house. No one responded. He went upstairs and checked the bedrooms and did not find anyone there either. He went to the garage and realized that Julianne's car was not there. She must have left to go to the store and maybe Gregory is with her. He still did not know if his wife was okay, thinking about the mess he discovered in the kitchen. He decided to phone Mark's house to see if Gregory was with him.

"Yes sir, he is here. I will call him for you," Mark responded politely. Gregory quickly informed his dad of the incident in the kitchen and told him that he would stay at Mark's house for the night. He didn't want to come home after the argument with his mother.

"I understand, Gregory. You have to remember that your mother is trying hard to be a better person and she is struggling with a lot of issues. I will speak to her tonight, but you have to promise me that you will come home tomorrow, so that all of us can sit down and try and have a decent conversation about everything that's going on. We need to work together as a family," Arthur explained to his teenage son. He knew that this was something that couldn't be fixed overnight but he still wanted them to try and get along with each other.

"I will see you tomorrow, Dad, I promise. I just can't be around Mom at the moment. She is still angry with me and I know her too well, it will upset her even more if I'm home tonight."

He could hear his father giving a sigh of disappointment on the other end of the line.

Gregory dropped the phone and knew that everything was not going to get better. If only his dad could see that, he thought to himself.

Julianne got home late that night. She finished her two beers at the diner and then decided to stop by the pub on her way home. There were a few guys who were nice enough to buy her more drinks and they laughed and drank until late into the night. When she suddenly realized what time it was, she quickly drove home before Arthur decided to come looking for her.

Arthur saw the car pulling into the driveway, music blaring out of the window, like a teenager. He knew then that Julianne must have gone out drinking again. He waited for her, sitting quietly in the dark.

Arthur suddenly felt a sense of relief to know that Gregory was not here to see his mother in such a state. Julianne struggled with the keys, she did not even realize that the door was unlocked, she was too drunk. Finally, she managed to open the door, came in, and took off her shoes, and started tip toeing to the kitchen. She knew that there was whiskey somewhere in the house and it must be hidden somewhere in the kitchen. She smiled at herself and walked into the kitchen.

Arthur walked quietly behind her. Just as she entered the kitchen, Julianne suddenly remembered what happened earlier. She switched on the kitchen light and saw that the place was clean. "Good! That brat better had listened," she said in a slurred voice. Julianne thought that Gregory must have cleaned the kitchen, as she instructed him to do, after all.

"No, I did," Arthur replied, still standing behind her. Julianne got such a fright, her whole body shook as Arthur started speaking behind her. She did not realize someone was with her in the kitchen.

"Arthur!" she yelled out in anger. "Don't ever sneak up on me like that again. You will give me a damn heart attack!" she continued yelling at him.

"Oh, I'm sorry, darling, didn't mean to frighten you, seeing that you are in such a relaxed state!" Arthur yelled back at her in a sarcastic tone of voice. "Look at you, drunk again!" Arthur was so disappointed in Julianne. His face was red with anger and he could not believe that Julianne went out drinking again.

"Oh, I'm sorry. Did I disappoint you, Mr. Perfect?" Julianne responded back sarcastically.

"Yes, you did, and you seem to enjoy hurting me!" Arthur replied in an angry tone of voice. He had reached the end of his patience with this woman. He couldn't take this anymore!

"What are you going to do about it?" she said, slurring her words and smiling at her husband, who had turned red in his face. He looked funny to her, maybe it was because she was drunk or maybe it was because she just didn't care for him anymore. He was right, she did seem to enjoy seeing him like this, all confused and angry, she thought to herself with a smirk on her face. Arthur wants to be in control all the time and the sooner he realizes that he can never control me, the better.

Gregory felt bad to leave his dad alone with his mother tonight. She was in a terrible mood when she left the house this afternoon and he knew that she would take it out on his dad if he did not go home tonight. It was already after eleven but he needed to go home, for his dad's sake.

He told Mark that he couldn't stay there tonight and he left, riding his bike home.

"Why are you doing this, Julianne?" Arthur needed to know why his wife was behaving like this. She was self-destructive and it was affecting everyone in his family.

"You have broken me, Arthur! You are not the man that you think you are! You are pathetic and old."

Julianne wanted to hurt him and she wanted him to feel the pain that she had been feeling for the past couple of years, since Ben passed away.

"You're drunk. I'm not having a conversation with you while you act in such a childish manner!" Arthur knew that Julianne was only saying those things to upset him even more and he refused to be part of her game.

He turned around and walked out of the kitchen. He needed to walk away before he said something that he might regret in the morning.

Julianne was furious. She wanted him to stay and fight with her and she wanted him to see that he was just as bad a person as he thought she was! He did nothing instead. He is such a wimp, she thought to herself. If only he would divorce her, but she knew that it would never happen because Arthur did not believe in that. She knew that she was stuck with him forever!

If she could be with Shaun, she would be happy again, she just knew that. The two of them would make such a happy couple. Shaun made her happy and he made her feel special. She wanted to start over, have a new life with Shaun. She deserved that. Julianne was sitting in the kitchen, having all these thoughts and then realized that if there were no Arthur, she would be a rich widow and would easily be able to persuade Shaun to give up his boring family to start a new and exciting life with her!

Julianne grabbed some meat out of the freezer and started to prepare a meal for Arthur. She wanted him to eat, sleep, and never wake up!

She was almost done with the sauce when she quickly grabbed her hand-bag in search of the prescription medication for her depression. She never took it because it made her feel funny and drowsy.

This stuff would knock out a donkey if you took more than the prescribed dosage, so she looked at the bottle and decided that Arthur was such a big ass, he deserved the whole bottle!

She smiled as she started crushing the pills on the chopping board in front of her. She added the fine powder to the sauce on the stove and put the lid back on.

In the meantime, Gregory walked through the front door, which was still unlocked. He could hear someone in the kitchen but decided that it was best to go straight up to his bedroom, which he did.

The meal was ready. Julianne didn't even hear her son walking into the house, she was too busy preparing Arthur's 'special dinner.'

The food looks delicious, she thought to herself. She took it upstairs to Arthur, who was in the bedroom.

"Arthur, are you still awake?" Julianne asked outside the bedroom door. No response.

She walked into the room and saw him lying in bed, watching television. "I'm sorry. I did not know what came over me. I had some coffee and I feel better now, see?" Julianne said in a soft voice, wanting to convince her husband that she was totally sober again, which, of course, was a lie.

"I even prepared you a nice steak to show you that I am really sorry about everything," she smiled and held the tray of food toward her husband. She wanted him to take it.

"We can't go on like this, Julianne," Arthur said, still angry at his wife, "I'm glad that Gregory isn't here tonight to have seen you in such a state."

Julianne completely had forgotten about Gregory. Good to know that he is not here tonight, she thought to herself.

"You are right. Please forgive me for behaving so badly. I promise. It will never happen again," Julianne said, trying to sound sincere. Arthur loved his wife and this was the first time in a long while that she had ever apologized to him, so he was sure that she must mean it.

"I would feel so much better if you eat something, dear," Julianne smiled and put the tray on Arthur's lap.

"Thanks, honey. It looks delicious," Arthur smiled and took a bite. In the early hours of the morning, Gregory was woken up by a strange sound coming from the bathroom. He got up to see what it was and what he was hearing. He walked past his parents' room and saw his mom lying in bed. The bathroom light down the hallway was on. He found his dad, white as a sheet, vomiting uncontrollably. There seemed to be blood coming out of his nose. Gregory immediately ran toward his dad and saw that he was violently ill.

"Dad, what's wrong?" Gregory asked in a panicked tone of voice.

"I think it's a stomach bug or something, Greg, don't worry, I will feel better in the morning." Arthur replied, not knowing what went wrong so quickly. One moment he was feeling fine and then he started feeling sick.

Gregory remembered the medicine cabinet in the kitchen and thought that there might be something in the kitchen that would help his dad feel better. He rushed to the kitchen and he saw that everything was cleaned up except for a sauce pan and the dirty chopping board on the kitchen counter. He looked for something that would help for nausea and found the medication in the medicine cupboard.

Maybe a glass of water, he thought to himself. He went to fetch a glass from the drying rack and saw the chopping board in front of him, he took a closer look, and he could see that it had white powder on it. It did seem strange at that moment but he did not give it a second thought. He needed to get back to his dad.

He ran back to his father, who had collapsed on the bathroom floor.

"Dad, please wake up!" Gregory was pleading with his father and he tried to help his father sit up against the bath, but he was unconscious. He had to wake up his mom.

He ran into his parents' room and there he saw the tray, on the bedside table. There was still food left on the plate. He picked it up and he could see that there was only one plate of food in the room. There might have been something wrong with the food, he thought to himself. His mother was still fast asleep under the covers.

"Mom, wake up!" Gregory shook his mom's shoulder in an attempt to wake her up quickly. She mumbled something and went back to sleep.

"Mom!" he screamed at her. She woke up with a fright and saw her son, standing next to her bed, looking scared and anxious.

"Jesus! You gave me a fright!" Julianne was immediately cross with him.

"Dad is in the bathroom and he is very sick. You need to help him!" Gregory yelled at his mom and ran out of the room again to go and check on his dad. He was sure that he could smell alcohol on her breath when she screamed at him. Maybe that's why she did not hear his dad being sick in the bathroom. She was passed out again!

Arthur was still unconscious.

Good, it worked, she thought to herself as she walked into the bathroom and saw her husband on the floor. She pretended to be concerned and walked toward where she saw Arthur, slumped up against the bath.

He was pale and there was white mucus in the corner of his mouth. Gregory was kneeling down, trying to wake his father up. Just as Julianne cracked a smile, Gregory looked up at his mom and saw her smiling and looking down at his dad.

"What have you done?" Gregory yelled out at his mother.

"What are you talking about?" Julianne quickly yelled back, trying to look concerned again.

"I made him dinner and he was fine when I fell asleep next to him a few hours ago," Julianne quickly explained.

"You are a liar. Dad was fine when I spoke to him on the phone earlier tonight. Now look at him!" Gregory yelled out, looking down at his father. He knew that his mother must have done something to him. "I'm calling an ambulance!" Gregory rushed past his mother to get to the phone in the hallway.

"Stop!" Julianne yelled back at him. "I can help him, I am a nurse, remember?" she rushed past Gregory, pretending to fetch medication for her husband. Julianne was well aware that her husband needed urgent medical attention, but she couldn't let Gregory spoil her plans. She knew that within an hour or so, Arthur would be dead and then all her problems would be gone.

Gregory watched his mom running into the kitchen and taking pills from the cabinet, "Wait here, I'll be right back. This should help." She showed Gregory the two pills in her hand as she rushed past him back to the bathroom. "You will see that he will be better in no time," she explained quickly. "Make me a cup of tea, will you?" Julianne instructed her son. She needed him to stay in the kitchen, away from the phone. She did not want him to phone for help, not yet, anyway.

"Okay," Gregory said, still not sure what to think of the situation in the bathroom. He had forgotten that his mom was a nurse; maybe she could help his dad. Maybe he was just over reacting. He walked toward the kettle and then saw the white powder on the chopping board again. He decided to clean the kitchen to help his mom while she was busy with his father. He opened the dustbin to throw away the onion peels on the counter and then he saw the empty pill bottle. He took it out and read the label. It was his mother's prescription medication for her depression. Her hand-bag was still in the kitchen and he walked over to look inside and found two more pill bottles inside with the same label on it. He took two of the pills out of the bottle and crushed it with a fork and then he saw that it was the same type of powder that was on the chopping board.

Gregory knew something was wrong when he saw it the first time. He looks around and did not see a second plate of food in the kitchen either, so why would she prepare only one plate of food? he thought to himself. He ran upstairs to his parents' bedroom and grabbed the tray on the bedside table. When he returned to the kitchen, he could clearly see the white powder on his dad's plate. He would not have noticed it in the dimmed light of the bedroom.

She poisoned him! Gregory thought to himself in disbelief. Gregory had had enough of his mother's nonsense and tantrums. She had caused the whole family so much pain and suffering. Now he was sure that his mother had started drinking again. She was obviously not taking her medication; the two pill bottles still full of pills proved that to him. His father must have found out somehow and that was why she wanted to hurt him. Well, this is the last straw! Gregory grabbed one of the pills bottle out of his mom's hand-bag and started crushing all the pills into a fine powder on the kitchen counter. He grabbed his dad's whiskey out of the cupboard and poured it in a glass. He added the powder to the whiskey and stirred it with a spoon until almost all of it was dissolved in the glass of whiskey. He quickly phoned the emergency services and informed them that his dad was very ill and desperately needed their help. He ran back to the bathroom with the glass of whiskey to give to his mother.

"I thought you might need this," Gregory said with a wicked smile on his face, handing Julianne the glass of whiskey.

"Honey, you are the best," Julianne could not believe that her son would bring her a drink, but she was definitely not going to refuse it now!

She smiled and gulped it down in two large sips, "Thanks, Gregory, you are right. I did need that." She gave the glass back to her son. Only then, she realized that there was something grainy in the last sip. He must have forgotten to rinse it out, she thought to herself. Never mind, she did enjoy the drink, and as soon Arthur is gone, she and Gregory might just get along after all, she thought with a smile. Gregory watched his mother closely. Just as he thought, she had done nothing to help his dad. The medicine that she took from the kitchen was still on the bathroom sink. If only the ambulance would arrive, he was not sure if his dad would make it through the night.

The minutes felt like hours while Gregory waited for the ambulance to arrive. Finally, the ambulance pulled up into the driveway. He quickly showed the paramedics to the bathroom where his dad was still on the floor unconscious. His mom stood there in silence as they carried his dad to the ambulance and rushed him to the hospital.

"Why did you call them?" she asked Gregory in a soft angry whisper, while they drove off with Arthur.

"You told me to, don't you remember?" Gregory lied but he knew that she would not be able to remember because at this time, everything must be a blur to her. She was still hung over from the drinks she had earlier that day.

"I did?" She asked him with a confused look on her face.

Gregory looked at his mom and said, "I think you must be very tired. Why don't you go lie down for a while, I will clean the bathroom."

Julianne looked at Gregory and thought that he might be right. Suddenly, she didn't feel so good and maybe, she did need to lie down for a while.

Gregory went to clean the bathroom where they had treated his dad. He wished that he could have gone with him to the hospital but he had to make sure that his mom stayed at home. She deserved what was coming to her.

Gregory took a quick shower and went to bed. He would ask Mark's sister, Lucy, to take him to see his dad in the morning.

Gregory woke up after a few hours' sleep and went through to the bathroom where he found his mother sprawled out on the bathroom floor. White mucus was coming out of her mouth and there was blood in her nostrils. He knelt down beside her and was not sure how to check for a pulse. He was not sure if she was unconscious or dead. She did look a bit grayish and felt cold to the touch.

He went back to his room, got dressed, and phoned the emergency services again, this time, hoping that they would take a lot longer to reach their house.

Gregory waited outside, trying to act anxious and afraid, as the ambulance pulled up again in the drive way. This time, police officers escorted the paramedics to the scene.

The doctor at the hospital informed the police that Mr. Smith had a lethal amount of prescription medication in his system and when they received another distress call in a matter of hours to the same address, the police had to investigate the matter further.

Mrs. Smith was declared dead on the scene and the boy was taken to the hospital to be checked out and to make sure that someone did not try to poison him as well.

Mr. Smith pulled through and after some investigation, the police informed Mr. Smith that his wife must have poisoned him deliberately after finding the plate of half-eaten food in the kitchen with the crushed powder clearly visible when the police investigated the scene. The police, then, believed that Mrs. Smith died from an overdose by talking a lethal amount of her prescribed medication with alcohol, which they found in her system. The police also found previous medical records indicating that Mrs. Smith had previously attempted to commit suicide and, therefore, they easily ruled her death as a suicide.

Gregory was clever enough to wash his mother's whiskey glass and place it back into the cupboard. This was what they did in the crime stories that he watched on television. He knew that his finger prints would be found on it if he left it in the bathroom and that would raise suspicion. Luckily for him, his father confirmed that Julianne went out drinking that night and that made the events fit precisely into place, just as the police believed how it all happened.

Arthur was thankful to his son, who had called the emergency services that night, and he knew that he would not have been alive today if Gregory did not come home that night. Gregory was very happy to see his dad alive and well when he arrived at the hospital the next morning.

He knew that from now on, everything would be much better at home. His mom was gone for good and his father would be happy again.

"I need to thank you for what you've done, son," Arthur said to Gregory while giving him a big hug.

"You saved my life, I am forever grateful for that," Arthur continued with tears in his eyes.

"I would never let anyone hurt you, Dad," Gregory replied softly.

"Sorry about your mom," Arthur said in a sad tone of voice. He still couldn't believe that Julianne had tried to kill him.

"She got what she deserved," Gregory replied softly.

Arthur did not hear the response of his son because at that moment, the nurse came walking into the hospital room, making a loud noise with the medicine trolley as she pushed it toward Arthur's bed.

"Sorry, you have to leave. Visiting hours are over," the nurse said in a strict tone of voice while glaring at Gregory.

Gregory just looked at her with a blank stare on his face. He could easily smash her head against the steel trolley and hide her body in one of the linen baskets in the passage, he thought to himself.

"Are you not listening to me, young man?" the nurse asked again, getting irritated with the teenage boy in front of her.

"Just take care of my dad, please, lady," Gregory said, looking back at the nurse. He had practiced this expression so many times and he noticed that it worked almost every time.

The nurse looked at the boy, who, suddenly, seemed so worried and scared.

"Sorry, I did not mean to frighten you. Of course, I will take good care of him," she replied feeling guilty for snapping at the poor child.

Gregory turned around and his expression on his face changed almost immediately, as he walked out of the hospital room.

"You better," he said while clenching his teeth. He could feel his hands getting cold again. He felt he must walk away and cool off. He walked down the passage to buy himself a soda.

If that nurse does not take good care of his dad, I might just have to come back and teach her a lesson, he thought to himself.

Gregory's dad was released from hospital a few days after the incident. Arthur was happy to be home with his son again, although he had to face the fact that his wife had taken her own life and that he still had to ensure that the funeral arrangements were made for Julianne. Arthur decided that a cremation would be best because he could then scatter her remains down by the lake. He was sure that Julianne would have wanted it that way.

Arthur kept a close eye on his son because he knew that this must have had been a terrible ordeal for a teenage boy to go through. The doctor at the hospital recommended that they both attend the support group meetings, which were held at the hospital once a week. The support group seemed to be a good idea to Arthur; however, he knew Gregory would need a lot more convincing before he would even consider attending it with his father.

Chapter Ten
A Long Night

Gregory was very excited to see his dad back at home again and seeing him looking healthy and much more relaxed made Gregory feel at ease. His father informed him about the support group meetings that were mentioned to him by the doctor, however, he did not see the need to attend it with his father. He was glad that his dad had found a way to deal with the ordeal, which he had gone through, and understood why he needed to attend the group therapy sessions.

On the nights that Arthur attended the meetings at the hospital, Gregory would invite Mark over for pizza or they would go to Mark's house to play video games. One of these nights, Gregory and Mark were walking back to Gregory's house when Mark noticed someone lurking in the shadows behind them.

"I'm sure someone is following us, Greg. This guy has been walking behind us the whole time and it seems as if he does not want to be seen. When we cross the street, he also crosses the street. When we turn left or right, he does the same. I'm telling you, something does not feel right with this guy behind us," Mark informed Gregory in a panic-stricken tone of voice.

"Are you sure?" Gregory thought that Mark might be paranoid because it was already late at night and he knew that his friend was a bit of a geek.

"Yes, just pay attention for a while and you will see exactly what I'm talking about," Mark replied very seriously this time.

Gregory suggested that they walk about a bit more, even though his house was just around the corner. He just wanted to make sure that Mark was actually on to something or maybe he really was just paranoid.

They crossed the street and walked toward the shop on the corner. Gregory looked in the shop window and he could see that the guy in the shadows was actually slowing down and noticeably looking at them from underneath his baseball-cap. Gregory went into the shop, Mark followed. They purchased one can of soda and some gum and walked out. Gregory looked down the street as they exited the shop, but could not see anyone.

"See, he is gone," he reassured Mark.

"No, he is not; you can see his elbow sticking out from behind the tree. Look again," Mark said, looking down while talking, trying not to let the guy know that he had spotted him in the dark.

Gregory looked and then he saw it. Mark was right. "Don't worry, we will walk straight back to my place and we will make sure that we lock the doors and wait for my dad to come home after his meeting. He can give you a lift back to your house later tonight," Gregory replied. He did not feel anxious or afraid. In fact, he felt a sense of excitement rushing through his body. They walked across the street again, toward Gregory's house. Gregory took the keys out of his denim pocket and gave them to Mark.

"Here, take this. Use this key to open the front door, walk in, and lock it behind you. I have a plan," Gregory said to Mark with a wicked grin on his face.

"What? Are you crazy?" Mark responded in disbelief. "You don't have to do this, Gregory. Just come inside and we can call the police if he does something stupid," Mark pleaded with his friend.

"Don't worry so much. I bet you that he will walk straight past my house when we enter the gate. I just want to see if I recognize him when he walks past the street lamp in front of my yard," Gregory explained. He knew that this was not the whole truth but that was what his friend could handle and that was why he told the lie. Mark reluctantly walked out in front of Gregory and entered the gate. He walked up the driveway, assuming that his friend was right behind him. He unlocked the front door and as he turned around, he saw that Gregory was no longer behind him. "Gregory!" he softly whispered, waiting for a reply.

No response. He was told to go in and lock the door, so that was what he did. Maybe Gregory went around the back of the house and would be at the back door, so he walked through the house to check if the door in the kitchen was locked.

Gregory was waiting quietly in a dark corner in his front-yard. He saw the guy walking up to the gate. The guy looked around suspiciously and quickly entered the gate. Gregory thought to himself that this was what he was waiting for. The guy had to enter Gregory's domain in order for him to act out his plan. You've overstepped a boundary,

Gregory thought to himself with a smile on his face. Finally, he could relieve some of this pent-up anger.

Dennis was sure that the two teenagers did not even notice him following them. He still had a grudge against Gregory for stabbing him with the piece of broken glass the other day. Thanks to Gregory, Lucy would no longer speak to him or let him near her and for that, Gregory had to be punished. He came prepared this time, his 9 mm was hidden under his sweatshirt and he also brought his hunting knife, just in case he needed it.

Gregory watched as the man walked up the driveway and then, he saw his face. It was Lucy's ex-boyfriend, Dennis. Oh, Dennis, don't you ever learn? Gregory smiled; he would definitely enjoy this fight.

Dennis quickly walked up to the front door and it seemed to be locked. He walked around the house to see if there might be an entrance in the back which he could use.

Mark was walking back toward the front door, after unlocking the back door for Gregory. He was sure that his friend would be here shortly. He must have had followed the stranger to make sure that he would not bother them. Gregory is like that, always taking care of people, Mark thought to himself, smiling.

Gregory followed Dennis around the house and he had his pocket knife already open in his hand. As Dennis reached for the back door, Gregory was inches behind him and with a quick move, he grabbed the gun out of Dennis' pants. He could clearly see the bump on the back of Dennis' sweatshirt and knew that it must be a gun. It happened so quickly that Dennis almost did not feel it being removed from his jeans. Then, as he turned around to see what could have happened, he saw Gregory's reflection behind him in the kitchen window next to him. Gregory quickly jabbed the gun against the back of Dennis' head. "Why are you following us, Dennis?" Gregory asked patiently.

"You think you are so clever, don't you!" Dennis hissed at Gregory, clenching on his teeth. He had had just about enough of this little brat. I will sort him out tonight! he thought to himself.

"Let's walk," Gregory softly responded, still jabbing the gun against Dennis' head. They turned around and walked away from the house. Gregory steered Dennis into a dark patch in the garden. Dennis swung around and grab Gregory's wrist. He was taller than Gregory and he knew he still had the upper hand in this situation. They struggled for a while and the gun went flinging through the air. Dennis reached in his pocket and quickly pointed the hunting knife toward Gregory. Gregory took out his pocket knife and pointed it toward Dennis. Dennis started laughing, "You are not serious! Do you think that your little knife has a chance against mine?"

Dennis could not believe the arrogance of this teenager.

"Oh, I'm sure it does," Gregory replied with a smile. Dennis looked at the kid standing in front of him, thinking that this kid is crazy. He took a step back and thought to himself that if he did not go through with this, he would never hear the end of it. This kid wanted to make a fool out of him!

Gregory could see that Dennis was debating whether or not if this was such a good idea.

"Come on, Dennis, are you a pussy all of a sudden?" Gregory taunted Dennis.

Dennis launched at Gregory with the hunting knife in his hand and with one movement, slashed through Gregory's shirt, across his stomach. Gregory could feel the sharpness of the knife on his flesh, but he knew that it barely went into his skin. He could feel his hands getting sticky and cold. The rush of anger went through his body and Gregory felt the urge in him grow stronger and stronger. He launched forward toward Dennis and slashed him on the forearm. Dennis looked at the wound and saw that it was only a minor cut and started laughing at Gregory. This was the breaking point for Gregory and he grabbed Dennis's arm and twisted it as if he was trying to dry out water from a towel. Dennis yelled out in pain and Gregory pushed him down on the ground, still holding his arm in a twisted position. He no longer had his knife in his hand. It must have fallen on the ground during the struggle. He left Dennis' arm and quickly scanned the area to find his knife. He saw the knife and Gregory stumbled toward it. Dennis got up and was rushing toward Gregory. He grabbed Gregory's shirt and pulled him toward himself. He quickly put Gregory in a chokehold and Gregory knew he had to fall to the ground in order to get his knife, so he did, bringing Dennis down with him. Dennis was now sitting on top of Gregory's back, shoving his head against the dirt beneath him.

"You little shit! I have had enough of you! I will teach you a lesson tonight!" Dennis kept on swearing as he threatened Gregory, grabbing his hair and continuously smacking his head against the dirt. Gregory could feel the knife next to him; he reached with his fingers and finally grabbed hold of it. He slightly lifted his arm up and shoved the knife into Dennis's upper thigh area. He quickly pulled it out and shoved it in again, this time, into another area in his leg. Dennis grabbed his leg and let go of Gregory. Gregory wiggled away from Dennis and he could feel that his head hurt from all the beating and that there was sand in his eyes but he could still see Dennis's frame in the dark. He quickly moved forward in the sand and stabbed Dennis in the back again and again and again until he had no more energy left in him. He did not even count how many times or looked where he had stabbed him. He just went into a frenzy and stabbed him everywhere and anywhere possible.

Gregory stopped, exhausted and out of breath, his hand was burning and throbbing. He looked at it and realized that he had cuts on his hands and it was bleeding. He could feel that Dennis was no longer moving underneath him. He did not care. Gregory quickly got up and ran toward the back of the house and went inside. He walked up to the front door and saw Mark, sitting on the porch, waiting for him.

He quickly ran back out through the back door again and jumped over the back fence. He ran toward the street and started walking back to his own house again.

Mark was getting worried because he was in the front-yard and did not see his friend. He wished that he would return soon, because Gregory's dad would be here any minute now and he did not know what to tell him if he asked where his son was. Mark saw his friend walking up the driveway, all bruised up and his shirt was torn.

"Gregory!" Mark ran toward Gregory and looked at him with shock. "Where have you been? What happened?" Mark asked in a concerned tone of voice.

"You were right; the guy was following us. I saw him walking up toward my front door when I yelled out at him and guess what, it was Dennis," Gregory explained.

"No way!" Mark could not believe this.

"Yes, he was still mad at us and he wanted to scare us. We started fighting in the street and he pulled a knife out and slashed me across my hands and stomach, see?" Gregory lifted up his shirt to show his friend the cut and he lifted up his hands, so that Mark could see the cut marks on Gregory's hands.

"You need to go to the hospital to have that checked out. Where is Dennis now?" Mark asked with fear in his voice.

"Well, I think that he felt good about winning the fight. He just left me, lying there in the street. Hopefully, we won't see him again soon," Gregory looked at his friend, smiling. "I don't need to go to the hospital, I just need to clean up before my dad gets home," Gregory quickly went into the house to clean up his wounds. He did not know if Dennis got up and left or if he was still unconscious in the backyard. He couldn't go check now. It would have to wait until he was alone again. He put on clean clothes and the bruises on his face could not be hidden away from his dad. He needed help.

"Mark, I'll take you home on my bike before my dad gets home but I need you to ask Lucy to fix my face."

The two teenagers quickly left on Gregory's bike. Lucy used all her make-up skills to conceal most of the bruises on Gregory's face. She had plenty of practice with this. They've decided not to tell her about Dennis because they did not want her to feel guilty about the whole situation.

They just told her that some bully attacked Gregory on his way home that afternoon and she believed it.

"I'm sure his face looks worse than yours," Lucy smiled at Gregory as she concealed his wounds with her make-up.

"He sure does!" Gregory responded with a smile, knowing that this was the only true part of his story. Gregory came home just minutes before his dad's car pulled into the driveway. He quickly greeted his dad as Arthur walked into the front door and went back to his room. He did not want his father to see him like this.

"Gregory, I bought some pizza on my way back, care to join me?" Arthur called out to his son.

Gregory hesitantly went through to the kitchen. His dad was sitting at the kitchen counter, busy placing two slices of pizza on each plate.

"Thanks, Dad. I'll pour us some milk to drink with that," Gregory politely responded and took two glasses from the cupboard. They sat and ate their food in silence for a few seconds and when Arthur looked at his son, he noticed that he had some sort of concealing cream on his face.

"Gregory, is there something that I need to know? Did you get into trouble at school today?" Arthur started, giving his son a chance to come clean.

"No, Dad," Gregory quickly replied.

"Well, then, what's that stuff on your face? Going through a phase?" Arthur asked with a sarcastic tone in his voice. Gregory did not think that his dad would notice the make-up on his face and he did not prepare any quick answer if the question was asked. "You can tell me, I won't get mad, promise," Arthur responded.

"It was just some stupid bully, Dad. He attacked me when I walked home with Mark. You don't have to worry, it's not that serious," Gregory quickly told the same lie to his dad which he had told Lucy.

"Are you sure? You must tell me if I need to go and talk to his parents. I will do that for you, you know that, right?" Arthur said, feeling sorry for his son who had been bullied.

"I'm sure, thanks, Dad," Gregory felt relieved that his dad did not push the subject.

They ate their food and talked about their day and went to bed. It had been a long night for Gregory.

Chapter Eleven
Getting Creative

Arthur got up and started getting ready for work. Gregory came walking into his bedroom and Arthur could clearly see the bruises on his face this morning because there was no make-up that concealed it.

"Jesus, Gregory, now that you've washed off that stuff, I can see that you took a terrible beating. Are you sure you are okay?" Arthur walked over to his son to get a closer look at his face.

"It looks worse than what it feels, Dad. I just want to ask if I can stay home today; I don't want to go to school looking like this. I'm sure that it will look better tomorrow," Gregory asked his dad, hoping that he would agree to let him stay home today. He still had something to sort out in the backyard.

"Sure, I understand. I'll phone the school when I get to the office and I will tell them that you came down with the flu. Just promise me that when something like this happens again, you will tell me so that I can help you."

Arthur gave his son a hug. He knew that this had been a tough year for the kid.

"It was a one-time thing, Dad. Don't worry, that kid won't do it again. I did fight back and I'm sure he learned his lesson," Gregory replied with a smile.

Arthur smiled and just shook his head. He knew that his son probably did fight back; he never was a push-over.

As soon as his dad left for work, Gregory went into the garden to check on Dennis. He was still lying in the corner of the backyard near some shrubs and bushes. As Gregory came closer, he could see that Dennis looked grayish in the face.

What to do? he thought to himself. He looked around and saw that there was a patch of sand where his mother's vegetable garden used to be. Gregory went into the garage and fetched the shovel to start digging a hole in the ground. Time to get creative, he thought to himself. It felt as if he was digging for hours on end, when finally, the hole seemed large enough to hide the body in it. He walked over to Dennis and started dragging him across the lawn toward the vegetable patch. Dennis' body felt stiff and cold. Gregory stopped next to the hole that he had dug up and tried to measure with his eye to see if this would work. He rolled the body into the hole and he was glad to see that it was long enough for Dennis to fit into the space. Gregory knew that this would start to stink up the place in a day or two and it might draw unwanted attention to it, so he had to go to the store to get something to help with his problem.

He quickly went in the house to have a quick shower. He got on his bike and went to town.

He explained to the shop owner that their drains had been blocking constantly and he needed something to disintegrate the stuff in the drain pipes and also something for the horrible smell coming out of the drain, which seemed to be a good excuse to purchase some lethal chemicals. He was given an industrial type of drain cleaner, which, he was informed, did contain acid and other harmful chemicals. He was warned by the store owner that only an adult should use this stuff and that the precautions indicated on the label must be followed precisely to avoid injury. Gregory reassured the store owner that he would never touch the stuff and he was only there to purchase it, not to use it himself.

Gregory got back on his bike and was happy with his purchase. He went to the home-improvement store and bought some easy mix cement, which he would put on top of the vegetable patch to ensure that no digging occurred there after today.

Gregory returned home and grabbed a clothing pin and put it over his nose because he knew when he would start to mix all this stuff together, it might just have a pungent smell. He also put on his mom's gardening gloves for protection. He grabbed a metal bucket out of the garage and placed it next to hole in the ground. He started to empty all the bottles in the bucket and mix everything together with a piece of pipe while looking down at Dennis, every now and again, just to make sure he does not start moving. If he does, I will whack him on the head with the shovel, Gregory thought to himself with a smile. He was right, the stuff did have a pungent smell, almost like ammonia, and he could feel that it started burning his eyes. He had to move quickly, so he started to pour the mixture over the body. As he started pouring the stuff over Dennis, he could see that it made little bubbles on the skin and clothing and then he knew that this would definitely work. Everything was poured out on the body and Gregory quickly started to cover the body with the pile of sand next to the hole. He went back to the garage to fetch the wheel barrow. He needed to start mixing the cement, so that he could cover the patch of ground today before his dad got home.

He followed the instructions carefully on the cement bag and the mixture seemed to be the right consistency. He used the shovel to scoop up the mixture in the wheel-barrow and evenly pour the mixture onto the ground. He took the shovel and tried to make the surface as smooth as possible. It looks great! We only need a small table and two chairs to put on this spot to finish it off, Gregory thought to himself, feeling relieved that he could clean up the mess before his dad came home today. He would show him his hard work and he was sure that his dad would like it.

Gregory was tired and hungry, so he went back into the kitchen and made himself something to eat.

He looked out of the kitchen window and he was glad to know that Dennis was dead and buried and would never cause Lucy or himself any more problems.

Arthur came home from work and he was glad to see that Gregory looked much better than yesterday. "I want to show you something, Dad. Come with me," Gregory took his dad outside and showed him the cement patch on the lawn. "I did this today so that we can have our coffee or breakfast outside, what do you think?" Gregory pointed the spot out to his dad. "It was mom's old vegetable patch, which she never really used and it was just sand and stuff, so I thought, if I do this for us, we can at least use the space in the garden. We can go to the store to buy a small table and some chairs and it will look great!" Gregory said looking at his dad's face, trying to see if he was pleased with it or upset.

Arthur was surprised to know that his son thought of this idea for the garden. "It looks great, I'm proud of you. You've done a good job, Greg," Arthur looked at his son with a smile. "Let's go buy the stuff while the store is still open."

They laughed and went to the store together to buy the garden furniture.

Chapter Twelve
Moving On

Months went by and Gregory noticed that his dad came home a bit later than usual, after the support group sessions at the hospital. When Gregory asks his dad about it, Arthur informed Gregory that he had met someone at the group meetings and he would like to introduce her to Gregory.

Gregory felt uncomfortable about meeting new people and although he was glad to see his dad doing better and being happy again, he did not want anyone else intruding in their lives.

That weekend Arthur decided to invite Margaret and Michael over for a barbeque at his house. Arthur had met Margaret at the group sessions and she informed him that she was divorced and had a son, named Michael, who was nine years old. She attended the meeting because she found it hard to cope with the fact that she had to practically raise her son on her own since the divorce. Michael's dad, James, lived with his new wife in another town and he hardly ever visited Michael, because he had a new baby with his new wife.

Margaret told Arthur that her husband had an affair with his secretary, Valery, and when she found out that the secretary was expecting James's child, she divorced him.

It was a messy divorce because Valery didn't like the fact that James still had financial responsibilities toward Michael, which is why Valery persuaded James to move out of town to start their new life, away from Margaret and Michael. She was sure that the distance between James and his son would do the necessary damage in order for her new family to get first priority in James' life.

Margaret and Arthur's friendship grew stronger and Gregory noticed that Margaret and Michael were at their house almost every weekend. Gregory knew that his father would meet new people after his mom died but he did not even consider the fact that it might be lady-friends. He thought that his dad would go out with his friends from work and that would be enough for him but Gregory soon realized that his dad was enjoying the company of the new lady friend in his life. As long as she did not try to act all 'motherly' toward Gregory, he would allow her to see his dad.

One Saturday evening, Margaret and Michael were saying goodbye and were preparing to leave. They never slept over at Arthur's house. They always went home at night when they came to visit during the weekends.

Arthur decided that he needed to have a talk with Gregory because he had grown fond of Margaret and he enjoyed having a young child in the house again. He wanted to prepare the spare bedroom for Margaret, so that Margaret and Michael could spend the night whenever they came for a visit again.

He knew that Gregory might not take this news well, but Arthur wanted to move on with his life and he knew that he wanted to spend it with Margaret.

While enjoying their Sunday lunch, Arthur looked at Gregory and knew that this might be the right time to bring up the subject. The two of them spent their morning buying tools and guy stuff at the mall and then returned home to prepare a nice lunch for themselves.

"Gregory, do you like Margaret and Michael?" Arthur started. Gregory looked at his dad and he knew what was coming next, he probably wanted them to move in or something like that. He hated the idea but he did not want to upset his dad.

"They are okay, I guess. Why?" Gregory responded softly.

"I was thinking of converting the study into a small bedroom for Michael. I want them to spend the night when they visit us on the weekends. I don't like it when Margaret drives home so late at night alone," Arthur thought that it might be a good excuse to convince Gregory to be on board with this idea.

"Oh, well, I don't use it, so it's fine with me, Dad. Just tell them not to go into Ben's room or touch the stuff in his room because that will really upset me a lot," Gregory responded, being very serious about this issue.

"Good Heavens, no, of course not! I will not change anything in your brother's room, as long as I can help it. He is always with us and I know this for a fact," Arthur smiled at his son, pleased to know that he did not forget about Ben and that he must also still miss him a lot.

"Good," Gregory said, smiling back at his dad. That went well; at least, he was not asking them to move in, not just yet, anyway.

After lunch, the two of them went to the study and started putting all the books and papers into boxes. They moved the furniture around a bit to make space for a sofa that could change into a single bed, so that Michael could sleep there on weekends. The room looked good and they were very happy with the transformation of it.

Arthur was glad to inform Margaret of the new room for Michael and he was excited for their next visit. He could hear that Margaret was upset about something when he talked to her on the phone and when he asked her about it, she informed him that she and James had a heated argument the other night and that Valery was trying to put a wedge between Michael and his dad. Margaret did not know what to do in this situation and Arthur felt upset because he did not know how to fix this for Margaret.

He went home that night still feeling upset about the conversation he had with Margaret. During dinner, he told Gregory about it, he was old enough to listen and to understand what Arthur was talking about; after all, Gregory turned eighteen a few weeks ago.

"Why doesn't she go over to that woman's house and put her back in her place?" Gregory asked while sounding very annoyed about this issue. He could never understand how people allowed themselves to be manipulated by other people.

"It's not that easy, Gregory. If Margaret goes over there, it might just cause even more problems between James and Michael. Margaret said that Valery is a bad person and she is keeping a close eye on everything that James does and she is trying really hard to create problems for Michael and his dad. The poor boy is only nine years old, so he does not know what the situation is really about and he just thinks that his dad doesn't love him anymore. The whole situation is sad, if you ask me," Arthur continued explaining to his son.

"Maybe you should speak to James about it, father to father. That might help, Dad," Gregory suggested.

"Believe me, I would if I could but James doesn't want anything to do with us. He is not taking it very well to know that another man is spending time with his son," Gregory responded.

"It might then be a good idea to stay out of it, Dad. I don't want anyone making trouble for you," Gregory said, feeling concerned for his dad. He worried too much.

Chapter Thirteen
A Fresh Start

Valery and James were enjoying a quiet supper in their house when James brought up the fact that he missed his son and that he might fetch him this weekend; he missed out on the previous weekend's visit because Valery begged him to go with her to her parents' farm, which they did.

Valery looked at James, she was burning up inside with jealousy and rage. How dare he bring up that little brat's name in her house! He had a new baby boy who he could spend time with and who would make him happy. She wished that he would forget about Michael for good! She and little Joey were his new family and that should be his priority.

The following weekend, Margaret and Michael came over and Arthur invited them to spend the night, which they did. Gregory was not home that weekend, he decided to go to Mark's house because was not in the mood for acting all happy and pleasant around his dad's new girlfriend.

Margaret walked down the passage and she saw the bedroom door with Ben's name on it. She felt anxious but curious to see what it looked like inside. She opened the door slowly and walked in. You could see that nothing had been moved or changed in years. The room was spacious and she thought to herself that it might be a good idea if Arthur moved all this stuff to the study, where Michael slept at the moment, and then he could use this room instead. She decided she would suggest it to him tonight.

Arthur just looked at Margaret with a blank expression on his face. How dare she even suggest that they move Ben's stuff out of his room? He could not believe what he had just heard. "That room will stay as it is, sorry, Margaret. It's Ben's room and I do not wish to change it, not now, not ever," Arthur stood up and walked out of the kitchen. He was no longer hungry and he wanted to be left alone.

Margaret felt guilty about raising the subject but it was also clear to her that Arthur might still have some issues with regards to his son's death. She did not need any more issues in her life, that was for sure. She followed Arthur down the passage, into his bedroom. "Arthur, I apologize. I did not mean to upset you or to sound ungrateful for what you've done for Michael. It was just a suggestion, that's all. I will leave, if you want me to?" Margaret said in an apologetic tone of voice.

"You don't have to leave. It's just difficult for me to talk about it. Please don't bring up the subject again. That's all I ask from you," Arthur responded with an annoyed tone of voice.

"Sure, I'll go make us some coffee. I'll give you few minutes alone," Margaret turned around and walked out of the bedroom.

Arthur knew that if he needed this to work, which he did, he would have to make some compromises in his life but this was one compromise which he was not willing to make. Not now, anyway.

Sunday afternoon came and Arthur said goodbye to Margaret and her son as they drove away.

He waited for Gregory to come home and the two of them went out for dinner.

He wanted to tell Gregory about Margaret's idea of the bedroom but he did not want to upset him, he wanted to tell him that he kept his promise and that no one would move into Ben's room. Maybe another time, he thought. It's not necessary to bring this up now, while we're enjoying the dinner.

As the months went on, Gregory realized that Margaret and Michael were at his house almost every other night. He knew that it wouldn't be long before his dad would tell him that they will be moving in permanently. Gregory was not thrilled with this idea but he knew that he just had to make the best of it, when that day comes.

The week before Christmas, Gregory was looking out of his bedroom window and saw the small moving van entering the drive way. He watched as the guys started carrying some furniture into the front door. There was a dressing table and chair, a double bed, which must be Michael's, a lot of boxes, and he could see that there were curtains and linen in some of the boxes. Gregory was sure that Margaret wanted to change their house into something totally different, something that was not even his style or his father's style, for that matter. He just knew that Margaret wanted to put her stamp on the place and that made him feel irritated and upset with her.

Gregory walked down the passage and saw Margaret, chatting with the moving crew and she was showing them where she wanted them to take the boxes and some of the furniture.

"Hi, Margaret," Gregory said, as he walked up to her.

"Hi, Greg, I did not realize you where home today," Margaret said with a hint of nervousness in her voice. She always felt uncomfortable around Gregory whenever he was around her and Arthur was not with her. This young man had the darkest brown eyes, almost black, and he always seemed to appear out of nowhere, she thought to herself.

"I do not know why you've brought your old stuff to our house. Where are you going to put all of it?" Gregory asks, sounding annoyed.

"It's not a lot of furniture, Gregory. It's just a few pieces of furniture that belonged to my grandmother and I do not wish to part with it. I've already sold most of my furniture after your father invited us to move in with him," Margaret quickly explained.

"You mean, moving in with us. I need to warn you, my father is not a huge fan of flower printed materials and I've seen the curtains that you brought with you. He won't like it, so don't even bother putting it up somewhere in our house," Gregory said to her in a stern voice, turned around, and walked off. He still couldn't believe that this was happening. He just couldn't get used to the fact that these two people would be staying with them from now on. Hopefully, his father would come to his senses and realize that he does not need this woman in his life; he could always kick her out again, hopefully, very soon.

Gregory went to Mark's house because he did not want to be around Margaret and her stupid kid the rest of the afternoon.

Margaret went into the house and started re-arranging the furniture in the living room in order for her couch to fit in the space. She also decided to use her curtains in the living room area, because it was bright and colorful and she thought that this space needed it the most. After all, they would be spending their afternoons in this area and at the moment, everything was gray and dull. She wanted to give it her feminine touch, which she did, with bright red and yellow scatter cushions and floral printed curtains. She did not care what Gregory thought at the moment, she needed to make this place her own and that's exactly what she was going to do.

Chapter Fourteen
Michael's Weekend

Arthur noticed that Michael was very quiet and kept to himself most of the time. He mentioned this to Gregory and asked him to keep an eye on Michael, he wanted him to feel welcomed in their house and he thought that the kid might still need some time to adapt to the new living arrangements and the relationship between Arthur and his mom. Arthur thought that Michael might feel more at ease to speak to Gregory about these issues, because it seemed as if Michael liked Gregory and did not mind being around him and talking to him.

Gregory assured his dad that he would look into this and that he would speak to Michael when the time is right. At first, Gregory decided to analyze Michael's behavior, this was something he enjoyed doing since he was a little boy. He quickly noticed that Michael's behavior changed whenever he knew he had to go and visit his dad and step-mom. This was odd to see because Gregory thought that the kid might have an issue with Arthur, however, the issue seemed to be with his own dad or maybe it had something to do with Valery, the step-mom.

Michael packed his back-pack on Friday after school because his dad would come to fetch him within the next couple of minutes. Gregory walked into the study, which was turned into a bedroom for Michael.

"Hi, kid. Looking forward to the weekend with your dad?" Gregory asked Michael.

"Yes, I guess so," Michael responded, sounding a bit off.

"Why the long face? Don't you miss spending time with your dad?" Gregory asked again. Now he knew, for sure, he was right about this. Something was definitely not right. "I am not allowed to spend time with him, so I don't know why my mom still bothers to send me over there," Michael said with a sigh and sat on the bed with his head in his hands.

"What do you mean?" Gregory asked, now very curious about this situation.

"Valery does not allow me to hang around my dad. She makes sure that whenever I'm visiting them, she keeps him very busy with other stuff," Michael explained further.

"You are nine years old and I'm sure you can go with your dad or help him, no matter what he is busy with," Gregory replied.

"You don't get it. She does not allow me near him!" Michael said, sounding frustrated, just thinking about it. "She only allows me to watch television with them for an hour or so and afterward, I must go to my room and play, because she and my dad must spend some time alone with the baby," Michael was sad and upset at the same time.

"That's bullshit!" Gregory responded in anger. Suddenly, Valery reminded him of his own mother,

Julianne. Gregory looked at Michael, sitting on the bed, looking so sad and pathetic. "Things will get better, you'll see. Valery won't be able to keep this up for long, I'm sure of it," Gregory responded and walked out of the room before Michael had a chance to say anything.

Michael's dad came to pick him up a few minutes after his conversation with Gregory. He was not sure what Gregory meant but he did feel better talking about this to someone who seemed to understand.

Valery was busy in the kitchen, making a veggie snack for herself, when she heard the car driving up into the driveway. It was James and Michael. She was in no mood for his kid today, but she had already made some dinner reservations for herself and James. The baby-sitter would look after Michael and Joey while they enjoyed themselves tonight.

"Hi baby, we are back," James said as he walked into the kitchen.

"What's for lunch?" James was hungry; he did not have anything to eat at work today. He was happy that Michael was visiting with them this weekend, he wanted to take Michael fishing tomorrow morning. He did not tell him yet, he wanted to surprise him. Michael walked in after his dad and saw Valery busy in the kitchen.

"Hello," he said softly.

"Go wash your hands, young man," she responded. She looked up at Michael with a false grin on her face, "So glad to see you again, kid." She was lying and Michael knew this. He wished the weekend was already over so that he could go home to Arthur and his mom.

"I've made us a salad for lunch. I've made reservations for us at the new Italian restaurant in town. I will ask the nanny to order a pizza for Michael while we are out," Valery said, smiling at James.

"Val, you know I wanted to stay in tonight to spend some time with Michael, watching movies and just relaxing in front of the television," James said while sounding a bit annoyed with his new wife.

"Oh, come on, you are always watching television during the week. Tonight, I want to go out and enjoy myself, so we are going out. That's it," Valery said. It was clear that there was no negotiating the matter.

"Call one of your girlfriends to go out with you. I will watch Joey and Michael. I'm not in the mood to go out, Valery. I've told you this already this morning," James was now angry. He decided he won't let her win this fight again.

"Fine!" Valery rushed out of the kitchen. James walked to the fridge and took out some cold meat and bread. He wanted a sandwich, not a salad. He was sure that his kid would prefer a sandwich as well.

"Michael, lunch is ready!" James called out to his son. Michael heard the argument and he felt guilty and uncomfortable to be here today. "Sit, let's eat," James said, smiling at Michael. "I'm glad you are here. I have a surprise for you tomorrow," James smiled again. Michael could see that his dad really seemed happy to see him and he immediately felt a bit better. He ate his sandwich and milk and was glad that he did not have to eat that salad. They played video games together for the rest of the afternoon. It was a good day after all, he thought to himself.

Valery went out a bit later on during the evening and he and his dad watched a scary movie and ate popcorn. It was great. Michael went to bed before Valery returned home from the restaurant.

The next morning, James woke up and started making sandwiches for them to take to the lake.

"What are you doing?" Valery said, as she walked into the kitchen. She came home late last night and they did not talk to each other after the argument they had earlier that day.

"I'm making sandwiches, we are going fishing today," James responded in a calm tone of voice.

"What?" Valery immediately sounded angry, "I'm not going to the lake! You know I don't like spending my whole day outside, getting bitten by insects and sitting in the sun all day!"

"That's your choice, baby. I am taking Michael to the lake today, I wanted to do this a few weeks ago but we had to go to your parents that weekend, remember?" James responded, sounding sarcastic.

"I'm taking Joey with me to my mom's house. I'm not going with the two of you," she stormed out of the kitchen and James could hear her slamming the bedroom door in the passage.

"Fine," he said in a quiet voice to himself. He knew that it would be an adjustment for Valery to spend time with Michael but it seemed as if she did not even want to make an effort to do so. He loved her but she needed to know that Michael would always be part of his life, no matter what. Michael woke up and went to the kitchen to see if anyone had prepared breakfast yet.

"Morning," he said as he walked in and saw his dad busy packing some lunch tins in a picnic basket.

"Guess what, we are going fishing!" James said with a huge smile on his face.

"Great!" Michael was truly excited. His dad promised him a while ago to take him fishing, but every time they wanted to go, something came up and his dad had to cancel the trip. Today would be a great day to go fishing.

They got in the car and drove off.

"What about Valery and Joey?" Michael asked as they drove on.

"They are spending the day with Valery's parents. It's just you and me, kid." James said, smiling at Michael.

"Great," Michael said in a happy tone of voice. Maybe Gregory was right, after all, things would get better.

Valery was still busy complaining about James on the phone to her mother. She was angry and upset because James did not go out to dinner with her and he didn't seem to care about her and Joey anymore. Valery knew that the bond between James and Michael must be destroyed in order for her and Joey to have all of James' attention and commitment in this family. She would have to come up with a plan and see it through for the sake of her and her son's future.

The day at the lake was great and James and Michael had a good time together. They did not catch any fish this time but it was still a lot of fun. They returned home early in the evening and decided that they would go home and clean up and then they would all go out for ice cream and burgers. They got home and Valery was already home. She still looked upset with both of them but Michael did not care, he had had a great day with his dad. He went through to his room and took a shower.

"Hi, baby, I think we can all go out for ice cream and burgers tonight. I'm going to jump in the shower quickly, get Joey's stuff ready. I will be with you in a few minutes," James said as he walked into their bedroom. He did not wait for a reply from Valery; he walked straight through to the shower.

"Sure," Valery replied as she knew that she had to pretend that she did not have an issue with Michael; her mother told her that if she did not play nice, she might just lose everything that she had worked so hard for in this relationship. So that is what she would do, even though she did not like it one bit.

All of them got in the car and drove off to have dinner together.

Michael was happy that the night ended without any arguments between his dad and Valery and she actually seemed to have calmed down a bit. She even smiled at him for a second, while they were enjoying their ice creams.

The next morning James got a call from the office and he had to go in to sign some paperwork and fax it through to the manager. He left early and told Valery that he would be home later to take Michael back to his mom's house.

"I will drop Michael off at his house if you want me to?" Valery suggested with a fake smile on her face.

"Are you sure? Only if it's not any trouble," James asked. He did not want Valery to feel obligated to do this.

"Of course, it's no trouble. I have to go to the grocery store, anyway. I will drop him off on my way to town," Valery replied.

"Thanks, babe." James smiled, gave her a kiss on the cheek, and left for the office. Valery was glad to have some time alone with Michael; she needed to ensure that he would not want to visit any time soon. Valery made some toast and eggs and called Michael to the kitchen for breakfast. "Michael, your dad had to leave for the office, so I will take you home after breakfast, but first, we need to talk," Valery said, as she pointed to the chair at the breakfast table, indicating to Michael to have a seat. "You know that your dad is a very busy man, right?" Valery asked. "His career is very important to him and his new family, which is myself and Joey. We are the first priority in his life and he wants to have a fresh start with a new and happy family, which does not include you or your mom. You are part of his past and your dad told me that he does not want any reminders from his past, when he was very unhappy. Do you understand?" Valery said, smiling, as she saw the expression on Michael's face change. He looked almost immediately very sad and confused. She enjoyed this and wanted to make sure that this kid would never want to set foot in her house ever again.

"Yes, I guess," Michael quickly responded.

"Well, he told me last night, when we got home after dinner that this was probably the last weekend that you could come and visit for a while, especially now that he has Joey in his life, which makes him very happy. He said that Joey was the perfect son. He did not know how to tell you this, so he asked me to explain it to you. You and your mom have started a new life with Mr. Smith and you must have realized by now that your dad has a new life as well, with me and Joey. So, you see, Michael, you will no longer come for regular visits because your dad would rather spend time with me and Joey," Valery smiled as she spoke to Michael and could see that the kid was nearly in tears.

"But my dad said that we will spend more time together, he told me this yesterday at the lake!" Michael responded in an angry and disappointed tone of voice. He could feel his tears rolling down his cheek as he spoke to Valery. This could not be true. Why would his dad hurt him like this, he thought they had a great weekend together and that everything was going to be okay.

"Sorry, Michael, you know your dad. He just can't be straight with people. He does not have the nerve to speak to you himself. That was why he took you fishing yesterday, it was the final thing he felt that he had to do. Joey needs him more than you do at this moment. You should respect this and let your father enjoy his time with his new son. If you love your father, you would respect his wishes and don't ask him about this, ever. If you do try to speak to him about it, it will be very disrespectful to him and your mother. You are old enough to manage without him from now on," Valery said, ensuring that Michael would not even consider the fact that he should speak to his father himself. "Eat your breakfast and get your stuff ready, I'm leaving in twenty minutes. You need to go home."

Michael felt his stomach turning and he felt sick. He wanted to scream with anger and wanted to see his dad and speak to him about this. This was the worst feeling that he had ever experienced. It felt as if someone had just told him that his father had died. He felt alone and confused. Valery dropped Michael off at the front gate and drove off to the mall. She had so much to celebrate today because, finally, she had James all to herself.

Michael walked into the house and went straight to the study. He slammed the door shut as he walked in. He dropped his back pack on the floor and started crying, it felt as if his whole world came tumbling down around him in a matter of seconds.

Margaret heard someone walking in the house while she was in the kitchen making some tea. "Michael, is that you? How was your visit?" she asked, glad to know that her son was safely home.

No response. Margaret walked out into the passage and heard that someone went into the study and slammed the door shut. She walked to the door, waited for a second, and then went inside. "Hi, Michael, didn't you hear me talking to you when you came in?" Margaret asked her son. She looked at him and realized that he was shaking, "Honey, what's wrong?" She walked over and tried to give him a hug.

"Nothing. Just leave me alone!" Michael responded in an angry tone of voice, still crying, while lying on his bed.

"What happened? Are you alright?" Margaret asked, concerned about her son. It was the first time that Michael had come home like this, all upset and angry. Something must have had happened.

"Just leave me alone!" Michael was angry with his mother, because now he understood what Valery said to him, he did not belong in his dad's life with his new family. He was stuck here with his mom, without his dad.

Chapter Fifteen
Speak No Evil

Margaret stood up and left the room. She decided to give him a minute to calm down and try again later to talk to him. Maybe he got in a fight with his dad about something and could still feel upset about it.

Gregory walked into the kitchen and saw Margaret, sitting at the kitchen counter, staring in to space.

"Morning," he walked past her and poured himself a cup of coffee. She looked up and saw Gregory, "Greg, can I ask you something?" Margaret thought that her son might talk to Gregory, instead of her. She would ask for his help and hopefully, will find out what made Michael so angry. He never talked to her like that, so something serious must have had happened at his dad's place.

Gregory looked at Margaret, who seemed upset. "Sure," he responded, while drinking his coffee.

"Michael just got home and he seemed to be very upset about something but refused to talk to me about it. Do you think you can try to speak to him? Find out what happened?" Margaret asked, sounding desperate.

"I'll check on him in a bit," Gregory responded. He was not in the mood to play psychiatrist today, but, what the hell, he had nothing else planned for the day so far.

He finished his coffee and walked through to the study. He opened the door and saw Michael lying on his bed. "Hi, man, heard you are back. So, how was it?" Gregory shot straight to the point.

"Go away!" Michael said, sounding irritated. Gregory looked at Michael and knew that something was wrong because he never spoke to anyone in such a rude manner.

"Fine," Gregory responded, walking out of the study. Michael sat up on his bed and watched as Gregory walked out of the study. He got up and slowly walked up behind him. He followed him into the kitchen.

"Gregory, are you close with your dad?"

Gregory did not even notice the kid walking up behind him, he quickly turned around and saw Michael, his face was pale and he could see that the kid had been crying. "Yes, we are. What's up?" Gregory asked.

"I was told today that I'm not allowed to visit my dad anymore and that he wants to spend his time with his new family. I'm no longer welcome there," Michael's lower lip started trembling and he was again on the verge of crying.

"What? That's bullshit. Who told you this?" Gregory knew that the kid must have misunderstood something, somehow. He had seen James with Michael and he could see that James enjoyed spending time with his son. "Valery told me that my dad asked her to tell me this today," Michael cried, as he played the image in his head again and again, hearing the words coming out of Valery's mouth.

"And you believe this?" Gregory asks Michael.

"Yes, because she said that my dad did not even have the guts to tell me this himself," Michael said angrily.

"I would not believe a word that woman tells you. You need to talk to your dad," Gregory advised Michael.

"No, I won't. He will just deny it. Valery said that he would not admit it because he does not have the guts to be honest about it," Michael was angry with his dad and he never wanted to see him again.

"Listen, kid, if there is one thing that I'm sure of is that your dad does not have an issue with you. Believe me when I tell you, you will know when one of your parents hates you," Gregory thought of his mom and he did not miss her for a second. Valery started to remind him of his mother again and if she was anything like his mom, he needed to sort her out quickly, before she ruined this kid's life. He did not really care for Michael, but he did care about his dad and if Michael started getting difficult because of his 'daddy issues' all of a sudden, it would create a lot of problems for his dad, which he won't allow.

"Tell me exactly what Valery has told you," Gregory sat down in the kitchen and listened as Michael told him about the conversation they had had this morning at James' house. Gregory immediately realized that Valery was busy with her own agenda. The kid was too young and dumb to realize that he was being played. It seemed as if Valery wanted to erase Michael from James's live for good and she thought that her plan would work. Well, she had got a surprise coming her way soon!

Gregory looked at Michael and replied in a calm tone of voice, "I want you to remember one thing, Michael. Since Valery moved in with your dad, she did her best to come between you and him. You have told me this yourself and if you think that you can trust someone like her, you are wrong. Did your dad treat you bad in any way this weekend?"

"No, we went fishing on Saturday and I thought that he enjoyed that. It was just the two of us. Valery and the baby did not come with us," Michael almost had a smile on his face again, remembering the good time they had at the lake.

"Exactly," Gregory responded. "I am sure she was probably pissed because you and your dad spent time alone together. Leave it to me, I'll sort it out," Gregory replied as he stood up and walked out of the kitchen.

Michael did not know what Gregory meant by saying that but he felt better talking to Gregory about it.

Gregory walked off to his room, leaving Michael sitting alone in the kitchen. It seems as if his Sunday won't be so boring after all! He grabbed some cable ties and duct tape and put it in his backpack. He took his Taser gun and a knife and put that in his bag as well. He left the house without anyone noticing.

Gregory drove up to James' house and waited for Valery to come home. He was waiting in the rose bushes for her to arrive. He had parked his dad's car a few blocks away, where it could not be recognized by anyone. He saw her car driving up to the house and the garage door opened. He quickly ran into the garage and waited in a dark corner. He was happy to see that Valery was one of those stupid people who opened the garage door before even entering their driveway. He pulled the ski-mask over his face and put on the leather gloves. He had a black raincoat on, which made him seem taller and a bit more muscular with black pants and black boots. He waited patiently; the Taser already in his hand.

The car drove into the garage and Gregory quickly put the oil can underneath the door, so that the door would not close completely behind the car. Valery got out of the car and unlocked the door that opened up into the kitchen. She was struggling with the shopping bags and did not even notice that the garage door did not shut properly. Valery hurried into the kitchen to put down all her shopping bags. He saw that Joey was still strapped into the car seat in the back of the vehicle. She went inside to put down her purse and would return to get the baby out of the car in a second. He waited a second and then rushed into the kitchen before she even realized that someone was behind her and jabbed the teaser in her neck at full voltage. He shocked her again and again, pushing the teaser into her skin until she finally dropped to the floor, unconscious. He grabbed the cable ties out of his pockets and dragged her motionless body to the middle of the kitchen floor. He tied her hands together behind her back and then maneuvered her legs to bend backward, tying them together as well. He then tied her hands and feet together with more cable ties. He shocked her again with the teaser, just to make sure that she would not wake up now, before he had a chance to finish with what he had come to do. She needed to be taught a lesson. He took out his knife and opened her mouth. He grabbed her tongue and cut off the front piece of her tongue, slicing through it like a piece of raw meat. He smiled as he looked at it. Hopefully, she would have a hard time talking shit from now on. He just laughed and stood up. He took the piece of tongue and shoved it down in the garbage disposal devise. The piece of tongue was shredded into mince in seconds. He looked around and took her wallet out of her hand-bag. He took the cash and credit cards, not that he wanted any of it but he knew he had to make it look like a robbery. He took her cell phone and placed it on the ground and started smashing it into pieces with the back of his knife. Gregory noticed that her ring looked pretty expensive, so he removed it from her finger. She had a gold necklace on as well; he took that from her body, so that it would appear that she had been robbed. He quickly went through the house and opened a few cupboard doors and drawers, as if someone was searching for valuable stuff to sell. Apparently, there had been a spree of burglaries in this area and he needed to stage the scene, so that the police would think that these were the same people who had committed the previous burglaries in this neighborhood. He had learned that the robbers usually run off with expensive jewelry and cash, so this was what he would take with him. He put everything in his backpack and looked at Valery, lying on the kitchen floor, blood coming out of her mouth. "From now on, you will think before you speak, Val!" Gregory had a wicked smile on his face, while looking down at her. He walked back out through the garage and crawled out underneath the garage door and kicked the oil can out from underneath the door, so that it closed behind him.

Gregory quickly moved in behind the rose bushes again. He took off his gloves, raincoat, and ski mask and put them in his backpack. He quickly walked out of the driveway, unnoticed. He got back to his dad's car and decided that he would keep the cash for himself and discard the credit cards and jewelry, because he did not want anything to be linked to him.

He drove home and parked the car in the driveway, where he had found it. He quietly went back into his house and he was sure that no one even realized he was gone for a while.

He went straight to his room and locked the door behind him. He took a pair of scissors and started cutting up the bank cards. He put the pieces in a small plastic bag and then in the trash can. He had already disposed of the jewelry as he was driving home, throwing it out of the car window near an alley. Some drug addict would find it and sell it for money before the police would ever get hold of it.

That night Margaret received a disturbing phone call from her ex-husband, informing her that Valery was admitted to hospital because she was attacked in her house when she returned home from the mall. Luckily, little Joey was still strapped in his car chair when James arrived home from the office.

The police had informed them that it must have been the same suspects who had been breaking into the houses in that neighborhood for the past few months. The police informed James that they will soon find the culprits and they will be brought to justice.

James begged Margaret that they should be careful and keep their doors locked at all times; he was worried for their safety as well. When Margaret informed Arthur and Gregory of the incident at James' house, Gregory looked at Michael and said, "You hear that, kid? See, your dad is still worried about you, even though you don't live with them anymore."

Michael just smiled at Gregory, knowing that it was true. He did not feel sad for Valery because she was mean to him. He was just happy to be safe at home with his mom and his new family.

Chapter Sixteen
Adapt or Die

After Valery was released from hospital, Michael was invited to visit his dad the following weekend. He enjoyed the peaceful atmosphere in his dad's house. There were no more arguments between Valery and his dad, probably because she still could not speak; he smiled as he thought about it. The doctors could still not give a full prognosis for her condition. They could not say if Valery would ever be able to speak again or not.

The weekend was great and Michael enjoyed spending some time with his little brother, Joey. Valery just sat in her room all day, which was great for Michael because the less he saw her, the better. He still had not told his dad about the conversation they had had the morning when she dropped him off at his house. Michael had spoken to Gregory about it and Gregory said that it was as if Karma came to collect from Valery. 'She had spoken such a load of rubbish, it must have been heard by the universe and it came to bite her in the ass.' Those were Gregory's exact words to Michael a few weeks ago.

"So, I think that you don't need to tell your dad about the conversation between you and Valery that day, it was already sorted out for you," Gregory just smiled at Michael and they both agreed to forget about the whole ordeal. After all, he did not want to upset his dad at this moment. He could see that it was very stressful for him to look after Valery and the baby.

The following months went by without incident. Everyone was happy within their new family environments. Michael and his dad spent every other weekend together and it felt as if Valery was only a figure in the background. It was clear to Michael that his dad loved him and Joey equally and he started accepting his new baby brother into his life. He would teach him everything a big brother should teach his baby brother.

Gregory went off to College and he only came home every other month to check in to see if his dad was still happy and doing okay.

All went well until Margaret decided that it was time to move Michael into Ben's room because he had started high school and she felt that it was necessary for him to have a proper bedroom. Besides, Arthur might appreciate having his study back for his work and his own privacy in the house. She decided to take matters into her own hands and started collecting boxes from the grocery store and where ever she could find empty containers. She would clear the room tomorrow after Arthur and Michael had left the house.

That afternoon, she took the boxes into Ben's room, so that they were there and ready for her to start packing tomorrow morning.

Gregory returned from college a day earlier than planned. He felt an urge to see his father and he decided to drive back home that morning. Margaret was completely surprised when she saw Gregory walking up the driveway, after being dropped off by Mark, his long-time friend.

As Gregory entered the house, he could hear that Margaret was in the kitchen.

"Hi, Margaret," he went in to great her politely, before he going to his room.

"Hi, Greg, you are home a day early, aren't' you?" Margaret responded, sounding surprised.

"Yes, I had to come home today. I just felt that I needed to do that, so I did," Gregory turned around and walked off in to the hallway. As he walked past Ben's room, he opened the door, as he had done many times before. He always went into Ben's room to say hi to his brother, acknowledging his memory and letting him know that he would not forget him.

The door opened and Gregory immediately noticed the boxes on the bedroom floor. What is this? he thought to himself. He looked around; making sure that everything is still in place, which it was. Nothing was moved or changed as he looked around the room, scrutinizing every corner of the bedroom, recalling every memory to ensure that all was still in order. He could feel his hands starting to get sweaty and cold and his anger was starting to rush through his veins. He turned around and saw Margaret standing in the passage, looking guilty.

"What are you planning to do, Margaret?" Gregory asked, the words almost inaudible because Gregory was now clenching on his teeth.

"I know that his was not my dad's idea. So you better start explaining," Gregory slowly started walking toward Margaret.

Margaret could see that Gregory was very upset and his face was as white as a sheet. He had the wicked expression on his face and his eyes were almost completely black. She started moving backward, away from Gregory.

"I… I did not want to upset you, Gregory," she said as the words came stuttering out of her mouth.

"You already have!" Gregory yelled back at Margaret and ran toward her. He would strangle her to death when he'd get hold of her and he knew that it would be all over within seconds.

She turned around to run away from him but it was too late. He grabbed her arm and spun her around, so that she could see him. He put his hand around her throat and lift her up with one swift movement.

"I will take your last breath from your body; do you hear me!" he yelled again in her face. "You have a choice this very moment, Margaret. Adapt to the situation in my house or die! Which do you choose?" Gregory was yelling at Margaret while pressing his hands around her throat. He could see that she was turning blue around the mouth and was near the point of fainting. He let go of her neck and she fell to the floor. He stood over her, looking at her with disgust.

"Which is it, Margaret?" Gregory wanted an answer now or else he would kill her.

"I will adapt, Greg. Please, don't hurt me," she started crying.

"If you ever come near my brother's room again, you will die. That is not a threat, but a promise. Do you hear me!" Gregory yelled at her again. His hands were clenched into fists. He could hear the blood rushing through his veins and pounding in his ears.

"Yes, I'm so sorry," Margaret continued to plead with Gregory.

Gregory turned around and walked off to his brother's room. Margaret slowly got up and walked toward the kitchen. She grabbed her revolver out of her handbag and quietly walked back into the passage toward Ben's room. She could hear Gregory was busy packing up the boxes which she had put there yesterday.

She slowly opened the door and saw him standing with his back toward her.

"Gregory!" she suddenly yelled out at him and startled him. He turned around. She fired two shots, aiming straight for his chest area, hoping to hit him in the heart.

Gregory fell to the floor. He could feel the blood, seeping through his shirt. It felt warm and sticky. What had just happened? Gregory fell to the floor and the last thing that he saw was the picture of him and his brother on the chest of drawers in the room.

Margaret went and stood over Gregory still pointing the revolver at him. "You see, Greg, I did make my choice. I choose to look after myself and my son. You don't know what I've been through the past couple of years. No one will come between me and my happiness, ever again! Not even you or your dead brother!" Margaret yelled at Gregory and pulled the trigger one more time.

Gregory just lay on the floor, motionless. Everything came to an end so suddenly and unexpectedly.

Margaret called the police and explained that Gregory had attacked her and the marks around her neck did not need much further explaining. The police concluded that the incident was definitely self-defense and that Margaret was free to go.

Margaret convinced Arthur to sell the house and start some place new as a family, which they did.